PIGGY TUCKER'S POISON

MALCOLM NOBLE

Piggy Tucker's Poison

Matador
9 De Montfort Mews
Leicester LE1 7FW, UK
Tel: 0116 255 9312
Email: matador@troubador.co.uk
Web: www.troubador.co.uk/matador

ISBN 1 905237 18 9

Cover illustration: © Photos.com

This is a work of fiction. All characters, locations and events are imaginary,
and any resemblance to actual persons, locations and events is purely coincidental.

Typeset in 10.5pt Stempel Garamond by Troubador Publishing Ltd, Leicester, UK
Printed and bound by The Cromwell Press Ltd, Trowbridge, Wilts

Matador is an imprint of Troubador Publishing Ltd

PART ONE

THE STRANGER

ONE

A Shop on the Nore Road

Widow McKinley's Curiosity Shop had been closed since Bugger's funeral. The black iron grill stayed locked to the shabby window frames and the plastic blinds, for years yellowed and cracked by the sun, now collected the dust of an airless room. Even the most curious of passers-by could not see inside. The shop was so run down that other traders wanted Maggie McKinley to sell the place so that something could be done with it. But the city folk who shopped on the Nore Road – at the greengrocers and butchers, at the haberdashery and the wet florist – didn't think that the little black and white shop was a blemish on the thoroughfare. Not a pimple, not even a prick. McKinley's had been there in the thirties; maybe the place was shut now, but it would come alive again. That was the way of things.

The old lady lived upstairs, in the front bedroom that overlooked the busy road and, although Timberdick said that she ventured out twice a week, no-one had seen her in the streets since May. Every day, she sat in her cluttered room and played Ted's old 78's. She liked to listen to the dance songs that he had sung to her before the war. She looked at the tradesmen in the street below and remembered how Ted had re-assured her about the changing times. "Never mind what the wireless says." He had a delicate, squeaky voice that fooled many people. "Things will stay the same for us. You look out of the window, Maggs, and count all the things that don't change. They talk of making tele coloured. What difference is that going to make to you and me? Take Telstar, it's three years old and we've nothing to do with it, have we? So don't worry." Here, he would clear his nostrils before going on. "I've heard our Timberdick tell you that reps in fast

3

cars do her well. Well, they're just commercial travellers, Maggs – just commercial travellers and they were the same before the war."

Ted had been right. Across the street, the poulterer still hung up his fowls before eight every morning and his younger brother, three doors up, still laid wet fish in the open and decorated them with shells and sprigs. Gilbert Brotherton, who always wore brown overalls, brought a van load of second-hand furniture to his corner emporium two or three times a week, just as he had done for sixteen years. "Another house cleared," Maggie McKinley muttered. "Another soul dead. But you'll not get my booty, Brown Gilbert. I'll make sure I'm sorted before I go."

It hadn't rained for weeks and it should have done if things were fair because poor Ted, the poor bugger, was a man who should be remembered in sad weather. But he had died at the beginning of the summer and there had hardly been a wet afternoon to match Maggie's mood since. She wanted to watch in the rain when the florist came out to her awning to usher the shelterers away and Barbara Bellamy stood at the window of her haberdashery as if she were mesmerised by water running down the glass panes. Malcolm the barber was always busy in the wet, Maggie noticed.

She had known the shopkeepers for years but rarely spoke to them now. The errand boys cycled past the Curiosity Shop without a glance. And the papergirl had nothing to deliver; Maggie had cancelled all that nonsense. The postman no longer brought letters to the front door. He walked down the covered footpath, minding the dog dirt and stubs of old vegetables (McKinley's was next to a greengrocer) and he poked any letters through the gap beneath the back door. Each time, he broke away a little more of the rotting wood but what else could he do? Mrs McKinley had no letterbox. When Timbers arrived, after hours, she would sometimes find a package wedged behind the chicken mesh that protected the little window beside the door. This was the window to the empty larder. When the back rooms were open for business, Timbers placed a dish of stewed prunes and a bicycle lamp on the cold marble slab. Then she would switch on the lamp and wait with the girls in the kitchen.

A dowdy policewoman stood quietly on the opposite pavement. She had been close to the little road junction for more than an hour, occasionally stepping fifty yards in one direction or another but always keeping the Curiosity Shop in sight. She should not have been there at all because a W.P.C. was not allowed to patrol on her own. But Miss Redinutt was a girl for breaking the rules. She knew that something was going on in there and she wanted to join in but, like a child in a new neighbourhood, she wasn't brave enough to cross the road and ask. If anyone had questioned her, afterwards, she would have been able to account for all the comings and goings. Not that there was much to tell.

The night had an uneasy feel, although the women could not put it into words for a long time. Did a girl shudder as she imagined the devil's hand on her shoulder? Did unnatural shadows fall from the grey clouds above? No, their nerves were not as tangible as those fancies. The haberdasher said, with hindsight, that the night had a waiting emptiness. Nothing was there when there should have been something. Weeks later, when people were dead and locked up and the detectives had moved on, the policewoman recalled her unease. She said, the Gods had gone to bed and left the back door open.

By a quarter to eleven the pavements had emptied and only an occasional car drove along the road. There was nothing but shops on the Nore Road and when the shops closed, people dried up like plants that come out only to be nourished. The evening was so quiet that, a hundred yards from McKinley's, a man could cross the road without looking.

TWO

The Walking Stick Man

The Walking Stick Man comes quietly but with the stage presence of a classical actor and no less confident of his place in the world. He is a large man, smartly dressed in new shoes, a creaseless raincoat and a felt hat that is deliberately two sizes too large. And in his left hand he carries a black lacquered cane with a silver handle. The handle is the shape of a naked woman bending over, so that the knuckle is her proffered bottom. As the gentleman walks, he strokes her intimacy with the pad of his thumb. It is a quiet eroticism, easily missed by an unschooled eye, but to others it serves to warn. The Walking Stick Man cannot breathe without an audience, he likes to think, so every stance, every fidget and quirk, is set to amuse and please. Like all practised performers, he knows the value of pause and silence. He knows not to compete with distractions so, when a noisy car goes past, he turns to look in a shop window. But for all his tricks of the trade, something says that this man has never been an actor. Perhaps he can exaggerate his own character but never assume another. Or does something messy in his past mean that no company would include his talents? So, where do his dramatic whims take him? He is too large to be a ventriloquist. He has neither the agility of a juggler nor the wholesomeness of a serious singer. No. He is just an enthusiast – a collector of theatrical goods, a lover of objets d'art, a raconteur without a real audience and no honest memories to his name. This man – the Walking Stick Man – is a fraud.

Widow McKinley watches from her first floor window but hardly notices him. She will tell the police that she was looking across the rooftops for the ghost of her husband. She had asked Timberdick to leave his supper in the coalhouse, so sure was she that he would come to her that night. Barbara Bellamy has moved her sewing machine closer to the window for light and she sees the gentleman. Days later, she will say that he looked like a man with nothing to do. He was window shopping, she will tell the W.P.C., but he was looking in every window, not just the ones that interested him. Perhaps he was away from home and wanted to kill some time before going back to his Bed and Breakfast. "Large. That's how I'd describe him. Tall and broad and weighty."

Should she say that there was something else about him? Something that made him apart from the rest of us. Something more than aloofness and eccentricity. Something that made her wonder what thoughts were in his head. But, 'he spent a couple of minutes at the electrical shop,' is all she will say. He was certainly interested in hi-fi. Then he looked at the grapefruit and bananas and when she looked again, he was gone.

Timberdick and Shannelle were cold in the kitchen. They had already drunk more coffee than they could stomach and the electric convector at their feet couldn't work for three minutes without overheating. Sitting each side of a light Formica-topped table, they had been playing 'scissors cut paper' because Shannelle said it would keep their hands warm. But Timbers had stopped the game when they made too much noise.

"Have you seen your Gordon?" Timberdick asked.

"He makes sure I do." The younger girl fidgeted with her new hairstyle. "He pretends to spy on me but he always makes it too obvious. He's thrown me out, Timbers, but he won't let me go."

Timbers offered a little bit of wisdom. "Shannie, we're never free of them. Men always come back to hurt you. They think they have a claim on us. Especially the bodily bits. We're like a farmer's field, Shannelle. Men come and have their picnics on us, leave their litter behind and, when they hand over a little money, they think they're taking out a mortgage. That's how they see it – and I guess they must be right because that's how it lives. Gordon's gone from your life, but he'll have left snares and traps to catch you out on dark nights. His name will be there – in years and years – like a threat or a price tag, or an unpaid bill in the post."

But Shannelle wouldn't have it. "I'd go back tomorrow, if he'd have me," she said.

Two years ago, Shannelle had shared Timbers' flat and some of their best mornings had started with them waking, one before the other, with daylight shining through the skylight above Shannelle's bed. Timbers looked older now – probably five years older – and Shannelle had changed. She had turned her hair mousy for 1965 and wore it short. The fringe wasn't really a fringe at all; it didn't lie on her forehead but came down the sides of her face like ill-fitting lobster claws. It made her look like Stevie Marriot in a pop group, she said. Timbers thought that it showed off her spots.

Shannelle conceded, "No-one else likes Gordon, I know that. You think he's creepy and he tells lies. I know that too."

"He talks in whispers, Shan, and he wears carpet slippers that his mother bought him."

"That's not true," Shannelle chuckled.

"Well, they look like his mother bought them. Shan, you don't know what he was like when he first came here, years ago. I'd put my arse up for sale and I'd see him, standing on the other side of the road, drawing me. Or I'd be drinking in the Hoboken and he'd be there again, across the room, working with his pencils and pad."

"A lot of men do that."

"But not like Gordon Freya," Timbers insisted. "He never asked."

"They never do. Not the real ones."

"Real ones?"

"Real artists," said Shannelle. "They never ask. It's the same with photographers on the street."

Timbers realised that her friend was relaying the explanations offered by her man. She wondered how many times they had argued about his voyeurism. She said, "But your Gordon made our skin crawl. All the girls said it. It was like he was trying to hurt you. Drawing was his way of taking you. Having you, without asking."

"Well, I've lost him now." Shannelle twisted a lock of hair around her finger as she reflected, "When he asked me to move in with him, it was the first time I had lived in a real house that didn't share any walls and had a garden. I didn't know if I loved him or not, but I knew that he was good for me and that felt enough. Really, it did. I cooked his tea and did his clothes like he wanted them. And I'd even spoken about having a baby."

Without meaning to, Timbers put a hand to her belly. Babies were something that she didn't talk about. She was thirty-five – too old, she thought – but, just recently, she had started wondering. Starting regretting, perhaps.

"Well, I've lost him now," Shannelle repeated. "He won't take me back. He always said he wouldn't if I started working again." She sighed, "How long are we staying?"

"We've not bloody started yet." Timbers got to her feet and ran the hot water so that the Ascot on the wall fired-up. She held her fingers in front of the inspection hole – the bare flames thawing her out.

Earlier in the evening, she had found an old fashioned dress, tossed in the corner of the junk shop. Now, she came back to the table, held the patterned cotton in front of her and tried to imagine how it could be worn to niggle at a man's senses.

"You know what Layna says?" Shannelle teased.

Timbers said she didn't.

"She said you look like a penguin on wheels." Shannelle giggled with all the naughty spite of a schoolgirl who has just told on her best friend.

Timbers smiled at the joke. She had cycled to the shop, her sticklike legs working ten to the dozen, and her cheap fur coat billowing like a pair of wings. So, yes, a penguin on wheels – she could see that.

The third girl clattered into the room. "Where's the bread knife?" she demanded urgently. Layna Martins was naked. Timbers had known her for four years but still gawped whenever she came near without her clothes. Her parsley patch was so glossy and had such growth – it was luxuriant. Everything about her looked so healthy. Her muscles were taut so that her limbs looked hard and fit. The moistness of her skin, the clearness in the whites of her eyes and the way her mouth always looked clean. And her breasts stood majestic, like no others. Timbers had tried to get her own to do the same in the mirror but Layna's out did them. Layna looked hand reared. "The heater's stopped working up there," she said. "And the knife's the only thing that'll fix it."

"You've left him alone?" Timbers complained. Time and again, she had told the girls off for leaving a man out of sight in the bedrooms.

"He's all tied up. He can't pinch anything. We're in the loft."

Shannelle grumbled. "No wonder the house is frigging freezing, you've got the loft hatch open."

"Bloody cold," Layna repeated.

Cold? But you are down here without your clothes. Timbers smiled at the contradiction. The vivacious minx knew that she was showing off. She had trotted downstairs to fix the heater but couldn't resist the opportunity to remind her classmates that she was the sexiest of them all.

"Don't worry about him. You'll not hear a squeak." She crinkled her nose. "He's a willy-white." 'Willy-white' was Layna's cruel corruption of lily-white. Taking something from lily-livered and Wee Willy Winkie, she meant that she was entertaining a weak cry-baby of a punter. The whiteness was especially barbed. Layna Martins was a good-looking brown girl. Her body was so shiny that it took on all the temptations of gold. "I dressed him in his stockings and corset and then, he says, he wants to be bound to the rafters in the roof-space. He wants the splinters to prick his bum, he says. Timbers, don't worry. He can't move, and a blindfold's over his eyes and ears."

Someone unseen tried the back door and the girls stopped talking. The caller tried again, then rapped on the woodwork.

The girls didn't move until Timbers decided. She threw the old fashioned dress at Layna and said, "Cover yourself up." Then she stepped into the little pantry and, with her funny face peering over the dish of stewed prunes, she looked through mesh that covered the little window. "We've not seen him before," she said. "Smartly dressed. Biggish." When she turned around, she saw Layna trying to stretch the dress across her chest and push it down over her hips. It would never be big enough and it went wrongly with the rich texture of her skin – but it stopped her being naked in front of the man at first sight.

10

Timbers collected the back door key from its hook. "You both ready?"

Shannelle said she felt all right. She sat on the edge of the table and started to cough. She always did and Timbers gave her a few moments to settle.

Timbers opened the door, keeping herself to one side, and the stranger walked into the scullery with a flourish.

"What crinkum-crankum goes on here!" he declared with thespian relish. He lifted his walking stick high in the air and Timbers' curious attention was drawn to the handle. The way that he twirled it made it difficult for her to identify the mascot straightaway. "I spy! I spy a dish of stewed prunes in the window. Ah, a woman who understands her calling. A stew-house! Let all men know they are safe in here."

For all the electricity that was going on, the girls kept quiet. Young Shannelle, with one cheek still perched on the table's edge, didn't know what to make of this larger than life gentleman. She knew he would be her turn because Layna already had a bloke and Timbers never went upstairs. So, Shannelle was the most available. She feared that, if luck were against her, she would be corralled with an unpredictable, hairy old stallion. God knows what he'd want to do with her. 'We can always say no,' she reminded herself. How many times had Timbers reassured her girls? It wasn't true; every working girl had known times when they had no say, and one look at Timbers' face told Shannelle that she would be allowed no choice if this impresario figure took a fancy to her. Shannelle shifted uncomfortably. She watched his thumb and fingernail play in the rude knuckle of the walking stick handle and she bit her lip. And, as she looked, the man said with a deliberation that made it fateful, "I come in search of Shannelle."

The girl's heart pounded.

Timbers said promptly, "Shannelle doesn't work any more. She's set up home outside the city."

"Ah, yes. She is Gordon Freya's woman. Don't you know that's why I want her?"

Shannelle's mouth went dry. This man wanted her only because she was Gordon Freya's woman. She was in his head, not because she looked nice or would make him feel good but because humiliating her would be like violating Gordon, like soiling his bedclothes. And this horrid man would have to make sure that Gordon got to hear of their encounter. No good would come of it.

He said, "My theatrical digs tell me that there's one here who knows her." Calling his lodgings 'theatrical digs' went with his fancied persona. If challenged, he would say that he meant his rooms were fancy and dramatic, not that actors frequented them. But the Walking Stick Man was never called to account for his words. He was so practised at building an image on a froth of half-truths that the weakness of it all didn't bother him. "One —" And he raised the stick in the air. "One — Timberdick."

Layna felt edgy. The gentleman had thrown her off the stage. Just two minutes ago, she had been flouncing around without her clothes, knowing that she had the best-shaped breasts, the tightest rump and perfectly muscled thighs. Now she felt like a rag doll. Her head was full of dark clouds that made her want to shrink within herself. The man was bad – a badness that brought perspiration to her palms and made her soles itch and her stomach feel empty. She sensed evil. There was wickedness in the room that her mother would have seen in pictures but Layna could only feel.

"Come now," he said, and Timbers watched his thumb working on the silver girl's bottom. "Why can't I see what's on offer? A parade of pretty maids, all three in a row."

Still, Timberdick said no. "We don't do chorus lines." And if we did, there would only be two.

Then he seemed to lose his presence as the lids closed over his eyes for a few seconds and he inhaled deeply through his nose. The comedy and the theatricals had gone. Mention of Shannelle's man had provided a glimpse of the visitor's dangerousness. He was a bad 'un on the prowl and Shannelle – and, yes, now even Layna – kept their faces down. They didn't want to invite his attention for fear that he might capture their souls just by looking in their eyes. He knew things. And so much in their lives could be dangerous to know.

Only Timbers looked him in the face. She was no more comfortable than the others but she took the blame for letting the Walking Stick Man into the house. She wanted to shoo him away.

Like a mother hen. "There's nothing for you here," she told him. The notion of Timbers as a mother hen was emphasised by the look on her face. She had bead-like eyes – pellets that stuck out from their sockets – and a crooked beak of a nose. She had no chin to speak of and, in the past year, she had developed a habit of tucking her bottom lip behind her two front teeth and ticking hesitantly. Like a chicken pecking at seed.

The man sat in Shannelle's chair and, as the girl was leaning against the table, she was almost touching his shoulder. "I have no intention of being dismissed. I came, honestly, to your stew-house. And that is all that I want. If I have suggested anything more sinister, then it is my performance that is wrong, nothing in my heart. What about this Little Nell?" He lifted the walking stick as if he meant to tap Shannelle's shoulders, but kept it short. "Is this who you are? Little Nell from The Curiosity Shop? Is this what really became of you? Never mind what old Mr Dickens told us. Nell is working in a stew-house, don't you know?"

Shannelle wanted to hate him. Oh, she hated him a little bit already but she was determined to hate him much more. Shannelle was the first to see through his acting. At first, he had wanted her because she was another man's woman. Now, he wanted her to play the role of a poor Victorian wretch. A hairy stallion? No, she decided, he wouldn't have the staying power of a stallion. He was flippant with his women. First this fancy, then another. He was just a Walking Stick Man. A promenader. She could feel the sweat fizzing on the tips of the pimples on her cheeks and everything that was wrong with her face turned red; that's how much she wanted to hate him. Yes, she'd take him upstairs and, almost careless of what he might do to her, she promised herself that she would humiliate him; she would be the better satisfied.

"Now then, my Little Nell." He nudged the end of the stick beneath her bottom and Shannelle wanted to turn and slap him. "You will tell me, won't you? Is your mother here, the one they call Timberdick?"

Shannelle did not answer him. She said to the others, "I'll take him upstairs."

Timbers, puzzled by the girl's change of attitude, studied

13

Shannelle's face before assenting. 'Who is this man?' she wanted to ask. 'Have you met him before? What's the history, Shannelle?' But Timbers gave up when she saw the girl's determination. Shannelle had something in mind. "Go on, pet," Timbers said quietly. "But no more than twenty minutes."

"Quite," said the man, with that smugness of a mature schoolmaster who has, at last, managed to introduce his class of dunces to the sunlight of knowledge. All along, he had known that he was going to get his own way. His thumb and forefinger were excited on the silver knuckle and the buzz transmitted down the walking stick so that it couldn't help but tap with glee on the scullery floor. Layna looked at the cane and saw an instrument of untold wickedness. She tried to catch Timbers' eye. She knew that Timbers was in love with her deep brown eyes and if Layna had been able to catch her attention, she would have been able to warn her. But it was all too late. The man and little Shannelle – she had always been the fat little piggy, too smelly, too farty and too hairy everywhere – they had agreed a match and the Walking Stick Man was shoving her up the staircase. It smacked of indecency – the man's eagerness and the inescapable picture of Shannelle as a sacrifice.

When they had gone, Timbers began to tidy the kitchen. She put the chair straight and filled the sink with soapy water. But Layna couldn't settle to a chair or the table, neither could she lean against the sink for more than a second or two. "I can't help it. It's so strong," she said.

"Oh God, it's not old gran'mamma's witchcraft again?"

"I can feel it," Layna insisted. She was tugging and snatching at the ill-fitting dress. "It's a wickedness that you've ushered into the house."

"Nonsense, I've done nothing of the sort."

"Lord above, Timbers, you almost curtsied when the Walking Stick Man came in. Like you were paying homage to the devil-man. You've drawn him in, don't you know that? All this leaving food out for Bugger McKinley's ghost and making a hocus-potion of stewed prunes and putting it in the window. The spirits are bound to notice these things, Timbers."

Timbers said that perhaps this visitor wouldn't be bad to

14

Shannelle after all. Yes, at first, Timbers had been thrilled by his sudden appearance at the stew-house door. Here was one of the old school. She told Layna about the Scotsman – big and powerful but gentle like this man – who had read the Bible aloud as she washed herself in front of him. "He called on me every month for three years and he never touched me. He never swore. He never grumbled." Perhaps the Walking Stick Man would be like him. She laughed, "Or the bank manager in his waistcoat, socks and shoes and nothing else?" He had been the one who told her to place a dish of stewed prunes in the window.

The telephone began to ring in the front of the shop. As Timbers stepped from one room to the other, Widow McKinley began to knock irritably on her bedroom floor. Timbers shook her head.

"I'll check my man in the roof, " Layna said.

"All right!" Timbers shouted into the phone as the banging continued. Then she heard Layna running up the staircase.

"What?" she said. The man had urgent things to say to her. "Wait!"

Mrs McKinley was shouting now as well as thumping. Then Shannelle screamed.

Timbers cupped a hand over her free ear. She needed to take in the message.

Both girls reached the bottom of the stairs together.

"Wait!" Timbers shouted. "Hold on."

"He's dead," Layna cried. She had the knife in one hand and blood was everywhere. "The Walking Stick Man is dead!"

* * *

The body straddled the bedroom threshold – his legs in the room, his head and torso in the passage. The side of his neck had been torn open – by a spike rather than a knife, Timbers thought – and blood had shot up the walls. His mouth was horribly open, as if the man's soul had been ripped from his body in one painful vomit. The hole in the neck was deep and open; the bloody membrane hung loose against the skin. It was like the crinkly plastic that butchers use to wrap giblets in.

15

"He pushed past me at the top of the stairs. He said he wanted to choose which room. He opened the door and just fell back on me." The words spilled out of Shannelle's mouth while her fingers gripped her jaw – as if some demon was speaking inside her and she wanted to shut him up. "Someone must have been in there. Waiting for him."

The women were standing in a queue in the narrow passage. Shannelle, then Timberdick, and Layna at the back. By accident, the smallest was at the front so each could see the body. Layna kept saying the blood was everywhere.

"Did you see anyone?"

Shannelle put her fingers in her mouth and shook her head.

"Layna had the knife," Timbers said, trying to get the sequence clear in her head.

"I dropped it when we saw him," Layna explained. "That's why it's covered in blood. God, Timbers, it's everywhere. How are we going to hide this?"

They weren't going to, Timbers had decided. She said, "Go through his pockets, Laynie. He'll have a door key. Nothing else, I should think."

"You can't ask me to do that!" the girl shrieked.

Shannelle stood still, open mouthed at Timbers' suggestion. "Layna will get covered in blood, Timbs."

"Look –" None of the women could take their eyes off the hole in the man's neck. "Look, none of us did this. Someone was waiting for him. That's what happened. So, we're going to explain that to the police."

"You're crazy!"

"I know what I'm doing. Too many people know we're here, and what we're up to. If we try to cover this up, we'll be found out. We didn't kill him. The police can question us, and then they'll know that we didn't do it. But, I want to keep one step ahead – so I need the key to his lodgings."

"I don't care!" Layna insisted. "Even if the police find out I was here, I've friends who'll hide me."

"Layna, you don't need to hide. You've done nothing wrong."

The widow started banging again. "You come here! You talk to me! I'm not coming out!" She sounded mad.

Shannelle said, "You do it, Timbs. You search his pockets."

"I'll get bloody and the police will know that I've tampered with the body."

Shannelle muttered, "Stop saying it," with her hand at her mouth. "Stop saying 'body'." Before Timbers could help, Shannelle's stomach came to her mouth; she turned away and she was sick. "I need to go downstairs."

"Love, sit on the top step," suggested Layna. But Shannelle was at the front of the queue and couldn't easily reach the staircase.

"Layna," persisted Timbers. "You're the only one who's got a reason to have blood on her hands. Please, go through his pockets."

"Don't be a cow, Timbs. Can't you see Shannelle's ill."

"We've got to do this," Timberdick insisted. "If we don't find out who killed this bugger, people will think we did. Do you think we'd work again? Do you think that the fresh faced, pimpled arsed, scaredy cat youngsters will dare to be alone with us. Of course not, they'll worry about their wives and mums and stay at home."

Some might, Shannelle thought. The weirdies would love the thrill of it. But Shannelle was in no state to speak up.

"And we'll be on the street corners again, hitching our skirts against brick walls for any Jack who gets out of his car and counts to a hundred. Do you think I'm going back to that?"

"Mrs McKinley won't let us work here anymore," Shannelle argued as she got to her feet. She was holding her sleeve away from her arm because of the sick on it. "No matter what. The police'll stop us, any case."

"So we've got to help ourselves. It starts with the key, Laynie."

With an impatient sigh, tall shapely Layna, still dressed in the ill-fitting frock, pushed her way to the front and closed her eyes tight as she stepped over the dead body. Her shoulders were already shaking when she knelt down; she was trying to keep her sobbing inside.

"Go gently now," said Timbers when the girl was in position. "One pocket at a time. Slowly, to make sure."

Layna got her courage together, then bent her head back, keeping her eyes shut. She pressed her tongue to the roof of her mouth so that her sobs came out as grunts through her nose. "Everywhere," she was trying to say. "Blood's everywhere." But the noise made no sense. Then she made a high-pitched whinny before pushing her fingers inside the dead man's trousers.

"Good girl," Timbers said softly. "Check to the bottom of each pocket."

Layna was crying. The big teardrops of a strong girl. The salt got into her mouth and when she wiped the tears away, she smudged dirty make-up along her jaw. "Timbers, why did you let him into the house? He's wicked." She pleaded, "Don't make me mess with a body that's evil."

"I've got to have that key. Go in with your fingernails pointing, yeah? You won't feel anything then."

"Stop being a bitch!" Shannelle pushed her face in Timbers' way. For a moment it seemed that the women would fight.

"It's here!" Layna exhaled and produced the Yale key from the first pocket.

"Right. Give it to me. And no-one mentions this. No-one says that we've got the key."

THREE

Peacock and Bloxham

Detective Sergeant John Peacock didn't want to be a film star because film stars only pretend. John Peacock was here for keeps. As he led Timbers across the Nore Road, he kept one hand loosely in the pocket of his John Collier jacket while the other explained things. He was short – surely too short to be a policeman, Timbers thought – but he was good looking in a tawny, fireside sort of way. Perhaps she'd like him one day, if he were honest. John Peacock didn't care what Timbers thought. Not at that stage. He was too busy walking. He knew that film stars who needed to play detectives would want to study the way he walked. 'The ease,' that's what he called it; John Peacock had 'the ease'.

Peacock had come to the city with a reputation as a detective who operated in his own way. He liked to work alone and kept away from police stations but because he had made his name in the country parishes of our police force, few of his city colleagues were ready to believe his stories. The D.C.I. paired him with Henry Bloxham and there was trouble from the start. Henry had joined C.I.D. late in his career, having pounded the pavements for more than twenty years, and this unruly Detective Sergeant didn't suit him. "We spend our time in the back of shops and sitting in the cars and we never go near a nick," he complained. "We could never account for how we spend our time." Now, I've never known a detective who wanted to account for his time, but perhaps Henry was more straightforward than the rest. He was a tall man with the neck and shoulders of a second row forward, and a deep lugubrious voice that made some people think he was slow witted. He looked as if he had stepped out of a Mickey Spillane novel. That's why they called him 'Hoodlum'.

Only Barbara Bellamy – the diligent haberdasher – saw the girls being escorted from the shop. She watched with the nosiness of a good Nore Road gossip but she saw nothing to alarm her. She guessed that Timbers and her chums had been arrested for keeping a disorderly house. Jolly good, and Barbara Bellamy promised to be in the front row when the court pronounced the punishments. But oh, poor Widow McKinley. For thirty years the woman had been bossy enough to defeat any scandal but her husband's death had sapped all her fight. The other shopkeepers wanted her out and tonight's bother would be their ammunition. Barbara resolved to congratulate the detectives for not arresting her.

They took Timbers to Peacock's Austin, parked twenty yards from the Curiosity Shop. It was two in the morning on a warm summer night with little damp in the air.

"You've got to talk, woman," said the big 'Hoodlum' Bloxham as he pushed Timbers into the back seat and opened the front passenger's door.

Once Bloxham had installed himself, Peacock said, "Get in the back."

"What do you mean?"

The Sergeant tapped his fingers on the steering wheel, keeping his patience. "I mean I want the lady in the front seat, with me, and you in the back."

"That can't be right, Serge. I mean, she's just a tart and I'm the policeman. Christ, I'd have to bend double to fit in the back." He was right; there was hardly enough room for his knees in the front of the car and the back seat would be even more cramped.

"Just move into the back, Henry."

Timbers leant forward from the back seat and folded an arm on the back of each front seat, then supported her comic-looking head between them. She looked this way and that, like a child following an argument between Mum and Dad.

"Look, we'll take her to Central and question her in the detention room."

"She's not a suspect, Henry."

"God, what is she then? The body was found in her bloody whorehouse."

"She's a witness and we're not taking her to a police station. Now, change seats with her."

Timbers waited. For a few weighty seconds, she thought the big fellow was going to refuse.

"Well, I don't see why I should," he grumbled, conceding. He opened the car door and extricated his large frame. He pulled and grunted and panted, but only for effect. Big Henry Bloxham was a fit man.

Timbers climbed over the seat, making sure that she put bits in Peacock's way as she managed her transfer to the front seat. First, she pushed her breasts against his shoulder. Then, when her knees were wedged between the dashboard and the gear stick, she stuck her bottom up to his face. And, when he didn't respond, she stuck it a bit further. She twisted herself and pretended to get trapped. She made sure that her blouse showed her tummy button. Then, with a final flourish, she landed backwards in the seat and let her legs fall wide apart for half a second, showing the crotch of her knickers.

"See what I mean," said Henry, from the greyness of the rear seats.

"I wasn't looking," Peacock said.

"She's making a clown out of you."

Timbers was quietly arranging herself in Bloxham's old seat with the smugness of a little schoolgirl who has got the better of her big brother.

"So where's your patch of pavement?" Peacock asked. "Outside the Hoboken, they say."

"She doesn't stand anywhere now," Henry replied. He took a box of matches from the side pocket of his jacket and, taking one stick at a time, began to split them and chew on the sulphur. "She sits in Heaven and makes the others stand for her. She's a puppet master. Grown up now, aren't you Timberdick? One of the top prefects. Head girl, even."

"Lay off her, Henry."

"Well, I can't see why I'm stuffed here in the back. You're trying to edge me out of the investigation, Serge. Just like always."

"Look, you're not going to pinch me for running a sodding cat-house, are you?" Timbers asked with mock weariness.

"For starters," Bloxham suggested. "It's not much but it's something. It'd wipe that bloody smirk off your face." Then, to his Sergeant, "She's got it all worked out, the smart arsed girl."

"Look. I'll show you my fronts if you let me go."

Peacock muttered, "Don't bother. Henry has already seen them."

"Bloody hasn't! Is that what he's said? Has he been putting the word about that he's seen me with my top off?"

"Everybody else has," Henry reasoned. He went on breaking matchsticks between his thumb and fingers.

"Well, perhaps there's a reason why you haven't!"

Timbers twisted around, easily getting her knees onto the cushion so that she could face the big man over the back of her seat. "Bloody pig! You" – and she started to pound his head and shoulders with her fist, – "Pig!"

"Come on," Peacock reasoned, but hardly moving in the driver's seat. "Leave him alone and turn round."

The blows continued. Timbers fought like a schoolgirl – scratching his face and the backs of his hands and trying to get at his hair. "I'll teach you!" she squealed. "Saying what you want to say about me, you bloody ape." Now she tried to get her feet on the cushion so she could get both hands at his throat.

"Christ, Serge. Serge, tell her."

The D.S. tried to grab the collar of her blouse, but it was like trying to catch an excited puppy. "Look, just settle down."

"God will get you, Henry Bloxham! We know what you like – God and I – and he'll put you in my way." She threw rapid punches and made noises from her puffed up cheeks like the pow-pow-pow of an ack-ack gun.

At last, Timbers plumped herself back in her seat. Then Peacock said, "Now, now, Miss Timberdick. Tell me again who has been in the house tonight. This time, Henry will write it down." Mention of his name made her fidget again, but Peacock put out a hand to steady her.

"You want to give us a couple of minutes, Henry?" he said.

"What do you mean?"

"I mean, go for a walk."

Without a word, the big D.C. got himself out of the car and

walked to a street lamp on the far kerb. Timbers watched him light up, his tough stance displaying his anger. Then he stepped slowly into the darkness.

The Sergeant cocked the rear-view mirror and fussed with his hair. "Henry is right. I should take you down the station, make you sweat in a cell until morning, then get the D.C.I. to question you, probably keep you until tomorrow night. Then, we could get a brace of D.C.'s to make sure no wayward husbands go near you on the streets. Awkward, really. Awkward for you." He was looking out of the car window, not wasting a glance on Timbers. "Or I could get you out of all that. Of course, that could land me in trouble with the Chief but I suppose I could put up with that. If I got the same favours as Henry-lad. Is that how it seems to you?"

She looked at him.

"With your top off," he explained. "Just for a couple of minutes."

She kept herself still in her seat. "You want me to take my top off?"

"Just for a couple of minutes. Hardly counts as much, does it?" He brought cigarettes from his top pocket, lit two and handed one to Timbers. "It was your idea," he reminded her.

Timbers kept her eyes away from him. She smoked, looking through the windscreen at the grey empty street, and allowed chestfuls from his quality cigarette to settle her temper. Now she wore the serious, reflective face that all her men loved. Timbers had short dirty-blonde hair, eyes that were too big for her face, a bony nose and no chin. She was scrawny and, when she kept quiet, she could look waiflike. She was a streetfighter who read romantic novels. She had been toughened by twenty years on the oily grit and dust of our back streets. She had learned that the world was a bad place, 'with no time off on Saturdays,' she often said. (Everyone should be able to do what they want on a Saturday afternoon, shouldn't they? Every child deserved that.) Sometimes, she got angry about the past that had brought her here. She knew right from wrong, she liked people and she didn't pinch. So she deserved better than this, surely? What did a girl have to do to get to Heaven?

She said, "I'm like a screwed up fish 'n' chip paper, tossed on the pavements. Blokes in this town take a good kick at me as they walk home from the pub. Here's old Timbers, the old tart, let's cross the road and give her a bashing."

"Well, are you going to do it?" he asked.

"Do you know what I'm doing at the moment? I'm sleeping in the church vestry because I've been thrown out of my own place. I've got no clothes to change into unless I borrow things from the other girls, and food's only what the do-gooders leave out for me. Twenty years in this city and that's the state I'm in. 'Get your tits out, Timbers.' That's all you can say to me."

"It was your idea," he said.

"You wouldn't say that to anyone else." She said angrily, "You wouldn't say it to Black Layna or Shannelle." She tossed her head, "Christ, you wouldn't dare say it to Layna. But you reckon you can say anything you like to Timberdick. God, you're in the middle of a murder case. You've asked me questions that you've got to ask. I mean, we know that you're going to let me go but you've got to ask the questions, just the same. I've told you everything I can about where I was and who I was with. And still you think 'we'll give it a try.' Let's ask Timbers to get her tits out. Like I say, you wouldn't say it to anyone else."

"Get on with it, then."

She drew heavily on Peacock's cigarette. "And look at this 'thing' coming on his bicycle. Great useless lump of lard. He can't even offer me a kip on his sofa because he's got some woman wedged stubbornly in his flat. Not even his doxy, she's not. A bloody lav-lady that he can't get rid of. What d'you think, Sergeant Peacock? Can you tell Stork from butter? Can you tell Ned Machray from a blob of grandma's lard? Teddy boys ought to rub Ned Machray's belly-fat into their hair on Friday nights."

* * *

When Chief Inspector Bernie Trent bought me my bicycle, I told him that I would never be able to cope with it. I had tried it in the country, I said, and I couldn't keep up enough speed.

"What do you mean?"

"Well, Governor, you need at least a brisk marching pace to stop

24

the wobble and I always run out of puff."

"That's rubbish, Ned. All policemen ride bicycles. It's what we do. You'll have plenty of time to practise on nights."

I have to admit that, as I pedalled up the Nore Road on the night of the murder, I felt that I was getting the hang of it. You see, big men like me make the mistake of sticking out their knees because, we think, we have to make room for our stomachs. But the secret is to raise the handlebars to their full extent so that your tummy doesn't lean forward. Of course, your knees still stick out a little but not so much that your boots slip off the pedals. Also, be economical. Only pedal when you need to. I found it easier to ride on the pavements. I thought that this would get me into trouble but, you know, folk soon accepted the habit. 'Here comes Mr Ned! Make room! Make room!'

I was approaching Barbara Bellamy's haberdashery when I saw two civilian cars parked on the other side of the road. I turned the cycle around. (I was well practised at this. Stop. Push backwards. Lean in. Crook the handlebars and press forward.) I returned to the zebra crossing. I was on the black and white patches when the first of the cars pounced forward and nearly knocked me off. I recognised Gordon Freya behind the wheel and, I thought, Shannelle lying across the back seat. 'Thundering idiot!' I shouted. "Think you're Stirling Moss, do you?" Then, just as I was getting the bike right again, old Widow McKinley ran in front of me. I nearly had her, I tell you. She was yelling and waving her hands in the air and looked scary – she was in her nightdress and mules and her hair was sticking up. She was calling for her husband, poor woman. I thought about catching up with her but when I saw her turn into Beach Road, I knew she'd be safe.

"For God's Sake, Machray! Get after her!"

D.S. Peacock was going to make many mistakes that night. I decided to let him off this one by pretending that I hadn't heard his instruction.

Bloxham heavy footed up to me. "Ned, you've got to stop him. Three girls and an old woman were in the house. And no-one else. And the black one had the knife that done it. And he's letting them all go. For pity's sake."

I liked Henry Bloxham. He had the old copper's way of taking his nose in his hand and reshaping it. With a snitching noise, usually.

"O.K." I said I would see what I could do.

Timbers was alone in the Sergeant's ice-grey Austin Cambridge. (He was very proud of it; he said it was going to be vintage one day.) She was straightening her blouse and putting her bra strap right. She looked like she had been in an argument and lost. Her large round eyes were staring into space and her face with no chin looked white and lifeless. She looked straight ahead, not at me. We hadn't spoken since my return to the city and a lot of resentment still needed burning off. I guessed that was the trouble.

"What are you doing here?" grumbled the Detective Sergeant. He was out of the car and smoking. "No-one told you to come."

"Keeping close to the gutter, Sergeant. That's what my Governor says. 'Get into the gutter and stay there, P.C. Machray.' I remember how he said it. Very serious, he was." I clambered off the bike and leant it against the Austin's very nice paintwork.

Then Ruby Redinutt came out of the house. She said that the Curiosity Shop was on her beat that night and the D.S. had adopted her as the 'fool-in-the-case'. No-one asked what she meant. Peacock complained, "You let the old woman escape, Ruby."

"I couldn't stop her," she said. Ruby had lost her hat and was clearly worried about it. She kept turning her head, looking for it. "She said she'd heard the ghost of her husband. But Sir, I don't think it was, Sir. I think someone's in the roof space."

The Detective Sergeant thought, nodded and trod on his cigarette. "You stay here, Timberdick," he shouted, tapping on the car window. "You're free to go. But wait until we get back. Miss Redinutt, run after the old woman."

I told them not to worry. She had gone round to Aunt Em's and she would be safe there.

"Do as I say, W.P.C. Redinutt. P.C. Machray, follow me."

The houses of murdered men have their own kind of silence. It's as if the departed spirit has taken away every emotion from the place so that things on shelves and windowsills, the out of place furniture, the clothes and the mess have no personality. It's as if they don't belong to anyone now. And if they ever did, well, they're not telling.

26

Clues? A flame hissed and popped in the Ascot. A chair had been overturned and three mugs were full of water in the sink. The larder door was open, but the only food was a dish of stewed prunes on the shelf by the little window. The light in the larder was off.

While C.I.D men notice these clues and write them down (some put lines and squares and boxes and triangles around them) true detectives get the clues to talk.[1]

"No clues here," Peacock said sadly.

The house had the dower odour of a guilty place. The Walking Stick Man had been a guest in an unfamiliar place and the house and its people should have done better. It was murder under trust; the worst of crimes.

I trod my dirty patrol boots over the scullery floor and up the stair carpet. "The girls are in the clear," the Detective explained. "The old woman heard the murder being done while they were downstairs. She banged her walking stick against the walls and that's what made them come up the stairs. She heard them. Layna Martins and Shannelle. Then Layna went down for Timbers. So, I'm letting them go."

"Sergeant Peacock," I began.

"John, please."

"Listen, John. You can't decide things like that. You've got to wait for a Superior Officer."

"If I'm wrong, the Superior Officer can put things right. I'm not a chap who waits around, P.C. Machray. Besides, it's too late because Gordon Freya has already taken Shannelle off."

"Which one was holding the knife?"

He thought for a moment, then said mistakenly, "Shannelle. All three said it was Shannelle. Definitely. She's a corker, that one. Fronts like two ice creams."

"Surely not?"

"Earthy, mind. That's the word, isn't it?"

Earthy, I agreed.

"And the black 'un's at Central. I've told them to throw her out."

"Layna," I said. "Her name's Layna."

---

[1] I didn't think that up; Chief Inspector Trent told me.

"I've always thought that was just her work name. They have more erotic real names, don't they?"

"Exotic, you mean."

"Machray, the E words are all the same to me. Erotic, exotic, erratic, et cetera. I can't tell 'em apart."

"Two ice creams," I observed in quiet reflection.

"Yeah. Like pointed cones, stuck on with vanilla splodge."

We were at the top of the stairs. It was difficult on the landing because a sort of tent had been assembled over the bloodied carpet.

I fought to keep my stomach in place. The man beneath the tent was dead in a brothel. People would say that he died with mucky pictures in his head; a dirty mind. But what did it matter? What's the point of behaving well if we all end up dead?

"Right," he said. "I need to get up to the loft hatch. Get a chair."

"From another room?"

"No. You're right; we'd better not disturb things. God, have you been treading up here in those boots?"

"It's too late now, Skipper." I said.

"Right, kneel down and let me climb on your shoulders."

I was bending down and he had one foot on my shoulder and another on my head, when I said I couldn't hold him any longer. "Stop complaining, Machray, I've almost got the thing open. Hell, Redinutt's a fool, getting me up here. I can hardly see, Machray. There's no damn light. What does she mean? Look, there's no-one up here; get me down."

He carried on talking as we got him back on his feet. "I haven't done anything with the body. Should I, Machray? What do you think? We've covered it up, of course and Redinutt had sent for an ambulance but I sent it away again."

I asked, "Our Ruby was on the scene?"

"Oh yes. Nore Road's her beat tonight. She was looking in the hi-fi window when the black girl ran out, yelling Murder! Murder! She hadn't got much on, she says. She must have told me that a hundred times. Oh God, Machray, I haven't sent for a doctor."

"Papa Alpha will have done that."

"Papa Alpha? You're up to date with these new call signs, are you?"

28

"Not really. I heard the young 'uns saying it, that's all. I don't do radio myself. Nothing wrong with an old T.K. Breath of life to an old copper, they are. Phone boxes."

We made our way out into the cold. "Erubescent," said Peacock. "It's another of those 'E' words. Some lad in the police canteen was saying it about his new girlfriend. See, they're all the same; words beginning with 'E' – they're all sexy." Then he stopped and stared at the empty car. "God, she's gone."

Of course she's gone, I wanted to say.

"Where's Redinutt? Why isn't she looking after her?"

"Because you sent her after Mrs McKinley."

"Well, Bloxham, then. Why isn't he here? Machray, I need dogs. And motorcycle checkpoints. And, what do you think? Oh God, Machray, it's all going wrong on me." By now, his cheeks were red and he was scratching his fingertips with his thumbnails. "Hell, Machray, I can't be here when the officers turn up. They'll think I've made a mess of things." A solution soon came into his head. "You stay here. Stand sentry. Take charge of the scene. I'm going to the station to see if I can round up the girls again. Take charge, Constable, until I get back" Allowing no time for discussion, he got into the Austin and started the engine. "If Bloxham turns up," he called from the open window. "Tell him I'm not here."

He was soon out of sight. I heard his gear change as he reached the Admiral of The Nore and I picked up the engine's hesitation (holding its breath?) as the car bounced over the Catholic School crossroads. Peacock had gone ahead without looking. I stayed in the middle of the road for a few minutes, then chose my spot in front of the shop's porch. I went 'uh-uhm' and assumed sentry duty. I kept my feet apart and my fingers interlocked behind my back. I did that policeman thing, lifting my heels from the ground every so often. Standing like a policeman is something I've always done well.

I was in charge, I reminded myself. In charge of the house, the murder scene – and that meant the body. Well, I was in charge of the murder itself, actually. The house, the scene, the body and the murder. I was in charge of everything and my bike.

Dorothy Rose 'Ruby' Redinutt came toddling back from Beach Road. She had the walk and the shoulders of a cross child. "He only said 'run after her' because he knew I'd look funny." She declared, "I can't run properly. I was the bloody pantomime at the police school. They used to make me run extra while everyone lined up to laugh at me."

"Be a lovey," I said. "Miss Bellamy across the street will be out of bed by now. Chivvy her up for a pot of tea."

"That'll make me a lovey, will it?" she said.

"But don't talk about the murder. Say Timberdick's been taken in for whoring. She'll like that."

Then, noticing that I was standing sentry, Ruby nodded at the shop and asked, "Is Timbers up there?"

"I should cocoa. She'll be a couple of miles away by now. She'll be on the sea shore, keeping a van driver occupied while others pinch his stolen fags."

Ruby's curly-topped head wobbled on her neck as she tried to work out what questions to ask. She said, "You know everything, don't you?"

"Enough to say that Timbers won't be hanging around here."

* * *

Upstairs, David Barton, the willy-white, was doing up his trousers in the dark. "How are you going to get me out of here, Timberdick? There are policemen and police cars and dogs. And my mother will know all about it by now. What are you going to tell the detectives, Timbers? The detectives are coming."

Timbers had decided that the widow's bedroom was the best place for Mrs Barton's boy to regain his dignity. Timbers stood at the window in the dark, keeping to one side so that she could not be seen from the street, while the fair-haired thirty year old put his clothes on.

"At the moment we've only a fat porker to deal with. We'll outsmart Ned Machray, no problem. But it won't be long before the C.I.D. come back, you're right. So, you've a last chance to tell me what happened, David."

The young man wanted to talk. "It was Layna's idea to tie me up. I didn't think it up. And the corset and stockings, too. They were

30

Layna's idea. She said that all men want to dress up, sooner or later, so I might as well do it tonight. And she suggested doing it in the loft. None of it was my idea, Timbers. Then she said that she was cold – of course it was, I had my clothes off and the trap door was open. Of course it was cold – so she went downstairs to get a heater. (Her idea. I didn't want to be left alone up there.)"

"So what did you hear, David?"

"Auntie Maggie came out of her bedroom and opened the sash window at the end of the landing."

"How do you know it was her?"

"Because she came from her bedroom. I'm definite about that. Then Gordon Freya climbed inside a few minutes later. It's quite easy from the coalhouse roof. I heard Maggie telling him that people should be made to respect Uncle Ted's memory. They should be frightened of him like they were when he was alive."

Timbers was still watching the street. "It might have been like that when he was young. But people had made fun of him for years. He was a dirty old man, David. Something you never want to be."

"Don't tell anyone about the stockings, Timbers," he pleaded. "They weren't my idea. I never asked and it was Layna, really. Really, it was her fault. She made me."

"Tell me about the killing."

He got his thoughts together, then started to explain. "I heard Shannelle and the man come upstairs."

Timbers interrupted. "Had you got free?"

"Yes," he admitted. "I was still in the loft and pretending to be tied up, but I'd worked all the knots loose."

"You wanted to fool Layna?"

"I wanted it to be fair and she wasn't being fair. She was making me do things. I was listening for her coming back, but it was just Shannelle and the man, at first. He said he wanted to look at the rooms. Then I heard him fall; Layna must have got to the top of the stairs at the same time. They screamed and ran downstairs. At the same time, I heard someone run along the passage and climb out of the window."

"Who was it, David? Don't tell me you didn't look."

"I was pretending to be tied up, wasn't I?" But he didn't stick to

31

his story. "All right. Yes, I did kneel down at the hatch, but I was too late. And I was only there for a second, Timbers, because I didn't want Layna to see that I'd escaped from the rafters."

"Now's the time for your proper escape, David. You're going the way Gordon Freya did, out of the sash window and across the coalhouse roof."

"They'll hear me," he argued.

"I'll be making such a fuss that they won't want to hear anything. They'll want to catch me. Now, you tell your mother that Timberdick looked after you, do you hear? You tell her to keep quiet. The police will hear nothing from me and if your mother and Auntie Maggs keep quiet, no-one will know that you were here when the murder was done."

*　*　*

Barbara Bellamy was carrying a tea tray across the Nore Road when I heard the widow's window open. Ruby Redinutt pointed to the sky. "Henry is on the roof!" she cried.

"Here!" shouted Timberdick, waving and reaching out of the window.

"Here," echoed the haberdashery woman as she offered the tea. She was too mesmerised to expect any answer.

The whole thing took on the sequence of a well-rehearsed drama. One thing followed another and we saw no way of stopping it. When Timbers thought that no-one had seen her, she leaned further and further out of the window. Rube thought Henry was losing his footing on the roof and shouted, "No Henry!" and that made Timbers twist around, look upwards and lose her balance. She tried to grab the window frame but the heel of her hand slipped off the cracked paintwork and she toppled forward.

"No!"

She heard "Timbers!" as she fell into the air. Pictures of tumbling trees filled her head. She knew she would hit the ground in seconds. She had no time to think about it. Then, beyond the last moment, two hands grabbed her ankles, snatching her fall with a jerk. She felt her backbone jar.

32

I ran to the pavement. "Christ, Timbers!" Even with my stretching up and her hanging down, there were unreachable inches between our fingertips. "Who's got hold of you?"

"I have, Mr Ned," called Aunt Emily's David.

"Then let me bloody go," shouted the girl. "I'm not hanging here like a noose from a bloody tree. My bloody skirt's up around my bum. Let me go."

"Don't!" I cried. "She'll crack her head open."

Henry Bloxham had rattled down the roof slates and only his knees in the guttering stopped him from falling further. "Don't move, Timberdick. I can get you."

"Don't you look, Henry Bloxham!" she yelled, upside down. "Don't you look up my knickers. God will punish you!"

I knew that I wouldn't be able to catch her if she fell, but would I break her fall sufficiently for her to avoid serious injury? I tried to work out what would happen, but only managed to get irritated by the useless dithering of the W.P.C. at my side.

"Good Lord, I have never seen this before," she observed. She was standing in the middle of the road, her arms limp at her sides. "Somebody actually hanging by her ankles from a window."

"Don't just stand there," I growled. "Get a box or something so that we can get her down."

"How long do you think she'll last?" she asked, not having moved.

"Get a box!"

"It's fascinating to watch. She's weakening. Can you see how her face has gone tight? Look, she's wincing."

I got angry with her. "Go and do something!"

A car drove at speed down the road, forcing the policewoman to jump out of its way.

Timbers felt her weight change as her blood fought to work upside down. The hands that were holding her were hurting her now. She started to swing like a clock's pendulum, her hands reaching for the ground in vain. Time and again, she wanted to twist herself free and only a last second's common sense stopped her.

Henry tried to secure his footing so that he could attempt to reach for her, but the old cast iron guttering threatened to crack. "Oh, help," he wailed and did nothing for the rest of the episode.

"Arrest him, Ned!" Timbers shouted.

"Arrest who?"

"Arrest bloody Bloxham. I can feel his eyes on my arse. Bloody theft, that's what it is. Taking advantage. Taking advantage without permission."

Then Barbara Bellamy came running from the other side of the road. "I've found the pole! I've saved the day!" She had collected the pole for her shop awning and, with a detailed commentary, hooked the eye of McKinley's shelter and pulled it open.

"Make sure you fall into the canvas when David lets go," I said.

"I'm letting go now!" he warned.

"Don't!" Timbers shouted. "I'm head first, for God's sake."

"Roll, Timbers. Swing and roll!"

FOUR

Changing Lives

"Your tart's put herself in hospital." Chief Inspector Trent shook his head, puzzled and downhearted. "She's no good to us there," he said. We were in Rennie Tegg's back room. The Chief Inspector was standing in front of a fire with a cup of tea in one hand and the saucer in the other. I was sitting in an easy chair, eating breakfast from my lap. Three fried eggs with black pudding on a good chunk of bread. Tomato sauce on one side and brown sauce on the other. I was saving the third egg for a cocktail of yolk and two sauces with toast dipped in.

"Things are no better at home, then?" he queried, as if my table manners were all the evidence he needed.

"I've still got the unwanted tenant."

"Fattie-Tucker, eh?" He took a sip of tea that was too hot for him. "Perhaps we can swap them. Get Tucker into hospital and Timberdick back on the streets. That way, you'd get the fat bird out of your hair and I'd get the job done. That's where we need Timbers, Ned, out on the streets. I want you to get down there, straightaway. Peacock and Bloxham are talking to her about the murder; she'll give them what she wants but not everything. We need to know who the victim was. He came looking for Shannelle, we know that much; and he probably knew Shannelle's chap, this Gordon Freya. But who was he? And where did he come from? Get those facts from Timberdick. Then stay clear."

"What has David Barton got to say for himself?" I asked.

"He was in the roof space when it happened."

"That matches W.P.C. Redinutt's report," I said.

"And he's detailed the events before and after the murder. If he's

35

telling the truth, our man was killed by Widow McKinley or the mystery man who left through the window."

"Probably Gordon Freya," I considered.

The Chief shook his head. "I think not."

"And if David's lying?" I asked.

"Then, any of them. The three girls, the old woman or whoever else."

"Have you spoken to Freya?"

The Chief Inspector was shaking his head again. "I agree with John Peacock. We don't want to bring him in yet, and he's a difficult chap to corner."

"He'll be in the Hoboken, after closing time, tomorrow night. Some sort of party about a painting, I think. Timbers could get talking to him, perhaps."

"Ned, I don't want you two messing around in this murder. You're working directly to me on the stolen cigarette case. That's why I've brought you back from the country patches. Understand?"

I nodded with my mouth full. (He didn't mean a stolen cigarette case. He meant the case of the stolen cigarettes, but I let it pass.)

* * *

1965 had started well for me. I had been sent to a New Forest inn where, because I was the only paying guest, I had the pick of the bedrooms. I chose the first floor front. It had a clear view of the village street and its green and the little lay-by where visitors parked before approaching the pub's porch. This was important because I had been told to look out for a Hungarian pair that was supposed to be meeting industrial anarchists here, or some other English tavern.

I liked the couple that ran the pub and before long I was lending a hand. I'd lay the log fire in the great hearth, provide an extra pair of hands in the kitchen or potter about the place with a screwdriver and chisel. Usually, I had run out of jobs by eleven. But lunchtimes were busy with local folk teaching me the funny ways of village life. And in the evenings I would play 501 with a man called Sam who told long stories in a Stanley Holloway voice. I'd get into bed at one in the morning, thinking how lovely it was not to work shifts. Every night I promised myself a lie-in. But at eight o'clock each morning I would dawdle down to the phone on the green and report, 'No Hungarians today'.

In February, the publican took me to one side and said that the Hungarians wouldn't be coming. They had heard that I had been sent to spy on them and had decided to do something else. He said, 'Your retired Commander has got it wrong. These are good people who are up to no intrigues.' Clearly, he knew more about the game than I did so I took him into my confidence, suggesting that there was no need for him to reveal that the game was up. Frankly, I was an old town copper who had suffered Sergeants and Superintendents breathing down his neck for years, so three or four months – or five or six – looking out from the window of a country pub was a welcome holiday task.

As winter turned to spring, I spent more time out of doors. I found a broken jetty at the bottom of the beer garden, and a dilapidated boathouse was on the other side of a narrow, weedy river. I set about repairing the wooden shack. I realised that I would be unlikely to finish the work but it seemed a more wholesome occupation than looking for phantom Hungarians.

It wasn't all hard-edged effort. I had already found a set of Jane Austen novels in the cupboard beneath the staircase. When the March breeze was easy and the ground not too damp, you could have found your overweight Bobby leaning his back against the old ash tree reading literate satire on English society. The publican's wife would set her record player on the kitchen shelf, throw open the windows and play Shadows 45's. 'It's Trad Dad,' she called across the lawn. It wasn't. 'Apache', 'Wonderful Land' and 'F.B.I.' were nothing like Traditional Jazz. But the catch phrase was the title of her favourite teenage movie, so whatever music she liked became 'Trad Dad.'

One evening a large man –tall and robustly built – took the corner bench in the public bar. His hair was white and wispy. (He would have looked better bald or close shaven.) His open cardigan, waistcoat, rough shirt and jacket gave him the layered look of a vegetable that had been left too long in the pantry. He wore a sad face and held his shoulders in a sad way. He said nothing but he kept his eye on me until I felt that I had no option but to walk over and introduce myself.

"Your London office thinks you should go back to Goodladies Road," he said.

I responded irritably. "I have no 'London office'. I have an old friend who sits at a dusty desk and telephones me when he thinks my life is too peaceful. I don't work for him and I've more than repaid any favours I owed him."

His face was hidden behind his beer glass. He took his time, then explained, "You won't recognise me. I'm Bernie Trent. A Chief Inspector from another force. Investigating a series of robberies from dockyard warehouses. Duty free cigarettes, P.C. Machray."

"Small beer," I said.

But he shook his head. "It's not straightforward. We know that the stolen crates don't come through the dockyard gates. They come ashore at different places around the estuary."

"So they're taken out to sea, then brought back."

"Thousands of them – and they all disappear down the Goodladies Road."

I said, "You want to talk to old Berkeley. He's a slovenly sod who spends hours in the branch library. He'll know all about the old smuggling coves. Or Fred Leaper, the railway porter. He's recently married a widow of a man who died on the lines. Not much gossip gets past Fred and his Mrs. Of course, your number one source should be Timberdick."

"That's why I need your help, Constable. You know these people."

"Why have they brought in a foreigner?" I asked.

"My appointment didn't please your Chief Constable. You'll understand that your City Division's in a mess, Machray. You know that. A thread of ineffective Superintendents has left too many questions unanswered. God, you'll have heard the stories – P.C.'s in brothels, W.P.C's in bed with all sorts. And your own Chief doesn't trust his C.I.D. to solve anything greater than bicycle theft. Lord above, you've solved the last two murders, I'm told."

Actually, I counted four. And Timberdick had done the detective work, not me.

38

"And when the Navy chaps ask for an outsider rather than the local men, well, the humiliation's too much for your Chief. Expect changes, Ned Machray. Expect changes. I'll talk frankly, Machray. Many people are relying on the Chief's daughter to put things right." He sniffed loudly and looked around the room. "You've found yourself a nice watering hole, Constable. You've had a good winter?"

I began, "I'm not sure how much you know?"

Everything, he said. He knew all of it.

He brought his beer to his mouth again, so that I couldn't see his expression when he said, "And that's not all. There's a damned pirate radio ship floating offshore. I've got to find out who's behind it." His comments had the telling ring of a phoney afterthought, but pirate radio wasn't part of my world so I let it pass. He put down his glass. "We'll have another, shall we?"

The Stew-house Murder was the only time I worked with Bernie Trent. I didn't get close to the man (we were each too private for that) and things turned bad between us before the end. But I liked the way he let matters take their time and he kept his detective work uncomplicated. Also, he was the only policeman to say that I was any good at the job.

We were both outsiders. The local detectives were suspicious of a man brought in by the Admiralty and when he asked for someone to pick up talk on the street, the C.I.D room (the sittingroom, we called it) chorused my name. 'Ned had a good war,' was the joke. But my Superintendent wasn't so ready to attach me to the new Chief Inspector. 'I've only just banished him to a country seat. Besides, he's doing something for his old friend in the War Office, isn't he? I'm not sure. Look, you must take responsibility for him if he comes back. He'll let you down. He always does. And he stays in uniform. I'm not having him plodding around my corridors dressed up like a Scotland Yarder.'

Over his second pint of beer, Trent said, "I'll need your help in finding some lodgings." He didn't want to rent a house and wanted even less a room above the police club, usually reserved for Superior Officers on detachment. "Get me near to the people, Ned. I want to hear them grumble about things. You know the sort; people who like a front door that opens on the street." He wanted to find a cosy sittingroom that he could use as his war office. 'A police station has more ears than a barley field,' he joked. So I had suggested that he should lodge with Rennie and Doreen Tegg. Rennie had been my tobacconist since I had moved to the city in 1936 and I knew he could be relied upon and provide the family atmosphere that Trent was looking for.

* * *

Doreen Tegg wouldn't be hurried. She worked the Hoover until the paisley patterned carpet had no more grubs to offer up, then she unplugged and secured the lead before wheeling the appliance out of the room. We thought that she might come back, so it was a few minutes before we spoke about the job. Trent went to his jacket pocket and produced a new packet of Senior Service. In those days, they were few more succulent experiences than the first cigarette from a fresh packet.

"What happened last night?" Trent asked, and blew quality smoke rings into the air. He was a skilful smoker.

"I came on duty at ten and got word that my snout wanted to see me in the Hoboken's back yard. He said that he'd give me information about a drop, just hours ahead, on condition."

"What condition? We don't let agents set conditions, Ned. You know that."

"He said he would give me the information if I promised to mess things up for the thieves. He wanted to keep his people out of trouble. Family, I guess."

"What do you mean, 'family, I guess'? 'Family, you know.' Stop playing games with me, Machray."

"He said a load would be coming in close to the yacht harbour at one. Two dinghies would meet it and take off the cargo. Except some amateurs from Goodladies had got to hear of it and wanted to substitute their own boat."

"While the first gang looked the other way?" he snorted incredulously.

"That's why they needed Timberdick. She'd be paid to distract them. In the way she does. He couldn't tell me where that distraction

40

was going to happen, so I decided to try the shortest way to the truth. I phoned Timberdick at the stew-house and asked who she was meeting at one. She would have answered me, Gov. It would have been just a normal job to her. Meeting a run of the mill chap. But before she could say anything, the murder got in the way."

He put the empty teacup on the mantelpiece. "Get the truth from her, Ned, and get your grass to tell us when the next drop is scheduled."

"And the murder, Governor?"

"Tell Timbers she's to give a statement to Peacock and Bloxham, then she leaves it well alone. Do you understand me?"

"I understand."

But the Chief wasn't so sure of himself. "I need to know the identity of that dead man. Why was he there? That's the answer to this murder."

"Yes, Gov."

I wiped the last of the egg yolk from my mouth and laid the tray to one side. "I'd better get going. I want to get to the hospital before lunch."

As I left the room, he asked, "What's all this talk about ghosts and ghouls?"

"Pay no attention to it, Gov. It's nonsense. People say they've seen Widow McKinley's husband on the streets at night. He's dead, Governor. Dead and buried." He didn't follow me through to the shop, so I supposed he was satisfied with my answer.

Rennie was wrapping four ounces of my Russian mixture in greaseproof paper. "Are you visiting Timberdick?"

"Yes."

"Will you be taking a gift? A box of chocolates, perhaps?" Rennie had come to this country in 1927 and had lost most of his European accent, apart from the hint of an 'ah' after words ending with 's'. If you looked closely, you could see his middle fingers lift when he said it.

"No."

"Do you think you should?"

"No. She'll have enough hospital food. Sweets'll make her sick."

"Well, I think you should take her some chocolates."

"Do you?"

"It's usual."

"Oh, go on, then, if you think so. Just a small box though, nothing fancy."

While he chose a large box and made a big fuss of taking a ribbon from a sweet jar and wrapping it around his selection, I was passing a pleasant minute or two looking at the smokers' paraphernalia in the glass display case on the wall. "Say, I'd like to look at these Maltese lighters," I said.

"Algerian," he said. "The enamel scenes are Maltese but the rest is made in North Africa. Sailors bring them in from the Med."

* * *

The big bosomed and heavy hulled Matron of St Agg's marched into the small side ward and declared, "Disgraceful behaviour!" She wasn't looking at Timberdick or the uniformed W.P.C. She was checking things – the picture on the wall, the neatness of the tablecloth on a corner table, the runners beneath the bed. She looked – and wasn't sure that W.P.C. Redinutt should be sitting in the upholstered easy chair. This was for visitors to paying patients, not for police guards. She tutted and continued her inspection. "Outrageous! And I cannot see how the night staff allowed you to get away with it." She ran a finger along the painted windowsill, checked it for dust or grime, and then did the same to one of the drinking glasses on the tablecloth. She ran her finger around its rim, then held it up to the light. "Utterly outrageous," she went on. "Ranting and raving in the middle of the night. Girls like you ..."

Girls like me, Timbers thought.

"You're nothing but trouble." Matron kept touching her spectacles as if she was unsure that they would stay on her nose. Timbers thought that she may have left her own at home and had borrowed a pair that didn't fit properly. "I've heard that one of my nurses had to lay across you to prevent you from getting out of bed and attacking the other patients."

It was like being snogged by a giant limp leek, thought Timbers.

"That's why they brought you in here." The Matron went back to the picture and righted it on the wall. "Not at all what our National Health patients should be taught to expect." At last, she turned to face Timberdick. "Any more nonsense from you and I'll send you for a rest in St Luke's." She could have been a camp commandant threatening a troublesome P.O.W. with the cooler. "Now, who is this?"

The W.P.C. got to her feet. "Woman Police Constable Redinutt, Ma'am. I was there at the murder."

The Matron grunted. "Unwise or unlucky? One is as bad as the other in my book."

Miss Redinutt went pink and, for a few seconds, winced Bunter-like as if her face had been slapped. "Timberdick hasn't been arrested, Ma'am. She's a witness the detectives need to talk to, that's all."

"I said, unwise or unlucky?" the lady demanded. "Lord, you girls can't answer questions, can you? I waste half my day, repeating simple questions because my nurses can't wash out their ears. And you can keep your smile to yourself, Miss Smarty-Tarty." Meaning Timberdick.

"The Curiosity Shop was on my beat, Ma'am. I was doing my job."

"Ah, so we're blaming the order of things, are we? Drop something and blame gravity, is that the way? Sit down."

Now, the Matron came to Timberdick's bedside. "I have sent a young boy away. He wanted to see you and I said, three o'clock's visiting and it isn't right for a lad to be wandering around on his own, here or anywhere. So, I've packed him off to the canteen and I've told the manageress to look after him. His mother can't be bothered with him, that's clear. His face is as parched and scabby as an elephant's hide."

"He has no mother," Timbers explained.

The Matron nervously adjusted her spectacles.

"His father tries his best, people say." Timbers shrugged. "I've never met the man."

"Well, I've arranged for a social worker to speak to the child."

"God, that's all the boy needs."

"His name?" Matron asked, tapping the fingers of one hand impatiently on the knuckles of the other.

"Didn't he tell you?"

"Not sensibly."

"Then he doesn't want you to know."

"The social worker will soon get it out of him."

"All right, I'll tell you his name, but keep the social workers out of it."

Matron eyed the bedclothes. "Has anyone been sitting on this?"

"Who could've? You've stopped people from seeing me."

"No visitors before three. The lad asked me to pass on a message. He said that he saw Digger McKinley's ghost last night, close to the Curiosity Shop."

"Bugger."

"I beg your pardon."

"He said Bugger McKinley. You said Digger."

"Digger, Miss Billie Elizabeth Woodcock, was what I chose to hear from a young child."

Timbers teased, "You're a very nice Matron. All the girls say so."

Matron turned her back and, pausing to adjust the picture again, walked to the second floor window. "I'd like you to see a lady from our clinic before you go."

"A doctor took my blood and wee last night. That's enough."

"All the same, I think a word with my lady."

"You think. I don't."

Now the policewoman coughed, rather timidly, behind the fingers of her left hand. "If Matron thinks you ought …"

"I won't."

"You should."

"Won't"

"Timbers," said Matron. "If you'll see my lady from the clinic, I'll cancel the social worker." She turned to face the room again. Then, without giving Timbers a chance to reply, she said, "And let that be an end to it," as she walked out of the room.

"Gosh, I can't help it." The W.P.C. took off her hat and ran her fingers through her hair to let some air in. "I just have to listen to big bossy women."

"Heaven help us," Timbers said quietly.

"Did you see her bottom? It's unusual for a big bottom to be so

44

firm." Ruby Redinutt spoke with all the authority of a policewoman who had studied the bottoms of older women. "Gosh, Timbers," she said, getting to her feet. "What's it like?"

"I think you had better cool off, don't you?"

"I mean, standing on the street corners, knowing that strange men can collect you at any moment. And not knowing what your next man will be like. Gosh. Look, I've got to tell you, I was sort of hanging around the Curiosity Shop last night. I mean, yes, it was my beat but perhaps I was there more than anywhere else. It's always interested me, you see, what you do and everything."

Timbers closed her eyes. "We'll talk later, shall we?" She was tired. Her little body had given out too much in the past twelve hours. Her gobstopper eyes ached and burned and her pug-like face looked drawn. In bed with her clothes off, her corner bits looked more bony than ever – her shoulders, knees and elbows – and her thin limbs looked more fleshless. If she didn't look sick, then she certainly looked weak and the wrong colour.

What was it like? She whispered, "It's having clothes that never fit you. It's being cold all the time. Even on warm sticky evenings, you're still cold somehow. You've always got stuff between your toes. Rainwater or mud or grit from your last bloke's car mat. And, no matter what they say, you always feel done down. It's horrible the first time a bloke looks at you – you're young and you think everything about you is bad – but then you get older and it gets worse. It's like people are always making a mess on you. Like, that's what you're there for. The girls who last are the ones that don't go rotten and don't get killed and start doing the mess on men. We'll talk later."

"Hey! That's Ned!" Ruby was looking out of the window. She may not have heard a word that Timbers had said. "Ned, wheeling his bike and talking to the gardener. He must be getting some flowers for you, Timberdick."

Ruby, you're a treasure.

I had found the hospital gardener, fishing green stuff from a lily pond, and asked him what to do with my bike. He straightened up, pressing the heel of one hand against his aching back. "Ah, good sense," he said. "Coming to Good Jolly and asking. If more people

45

would do it, less people would lose their bicycles." He walked me to a shed full of wheelbarrows and invited me to chain the bike to a great iron cartwheel. This took me a few minutes – because padlocks and chains are not easy things for me to manage – and when I looked around, he had gathered a bunch of flowers. "Here, you'll want these. Asking, you see. That makes the difference."

A Sister recognised me on the ground floor and took me into the lift. "We had a little trouble with her during the night," she reported. "She was shouting at other patients and wanted to fight the night nurses. We had to trolley her into a side ward. You should have seen it, Mr Machray. Quite, quite, 'Doctor in the House', it was."

As I walked into the little white room, Timbers said, "I've got to talk to you, Ned."

"You're in trouble, Timbers." I warned.

"I've got to talk to you," she repeated.

She asked Ruby to step outside. When the girl dithered, Timbers told her off, good and proper. "You think you're a detective, do you? Too important to do what you're told. Well, I'll say this to you, young woman. You messed up the whole job at Mrs McKinley's place. You were told to stand sentry but more people were dropping in and out of that back door than Clarence Pier's lavs on a dirty Friday night. Now, if you listen to me, take it in and do as I say – I might, I just might be able to fix things for you. So now, get out."

"That's not fair!"

"Yes, it is," Timbers insisted. "Poor Ned wants me to tell him my secrets. On our own, Rube."

Ruby hung her head and coughed behind proffered fingers. She mumbled about fairness and wanting to be friends with everyone, then she backed away, through the door. (The next time I saw her, she was sulking in the hospital canteen.)

"Did you have to be so sharp?" I asked Timberdick.

"The girl needs to slow down," Timbers explained. Her head lolled on her shoulders and I saw how tired she was. Putting things right between us would have to wait. Her funny face went dreamy as she said, "Now, Ned, things aren't as Widow McKinley said. Ned, I can't say that Shannelle or Layna didn't murder the man. Ned, they could have done it."

46

I laid the flowers on the hospital counterpane, not really knowing what to do with them. I sat on the bottom of the bed and said, "You'd better talk me through it." I pulled the ribbons off the chocolate box and peeped inside.

"The Matron won't like it," Timbers warned. "She plays up if anyone sits on the blankets."

"Did you know who the dead man was?"

Timbers shook her head. "Is the Toilet Brush still with you?"

"Where did he come from, Timbers? Where was he staying? Digs? A Bed and Breakfast? The lads found no keys on him."

"What makes you think I know him?" she asked.

"He knew Gordon Freya. You told Peacock that much. You said he was looking for Shannelle because she was Gordon Freya's girlfriend. So, who is he? What's it about?" I knew she wasn't going to answer my questions, so I opened the chocolates. "Let's go through it. I phoned you about twenty past eleven." I popped a coffee cream in my mouth. "You'd like these," I said.

"Why'd you do that? Why did you phone? Is the Toilet Brush still with you?"

"You know she is, Timbers," I said as I munched. "I can't get rid of her."

"Tell her to be careful, Ned. Some of the girls are thinking maybe she needs to be taught a lesson. Crowding our policeman and making a burden of herself. She didn't ought to get away with it, they're saying."

"Now, we'll have no more talk like that," I cautioned. "We're supposed to be talking about the murder. What was going on when I phoned?"

"The dead man walked up the stairs first. Shannelle was so close behind him that she could have been pushing his bum. She says, she showed him into the little bedroom, and then she came back to the top of the stairs and called for Layna. She needed the knife to fix the heater."

"So the dead man was alone in the bedroom?"

"Except he wasn't dead yet."

"I agree – but he was alone."

"For less than a minute, Ned. Oh God, can't you finish one

47

before you start another. You're like a kid; you've got chocolate all over your fingers."

"I know. I know," I said and licked the ends. "Let's look at this. Layna didn't go upstairs immediately, did she? I telephoned and I didn't hear Shannelle calling."

"No, she shouted just before the phone started ringing."

"And you had to walk from the kitchen to the shop before you could answer it. We spoke to each other and then the banging started."

Timbers agreed. "That was Mrs McKinley upstairs."

"Then I heard Layna telling you that she was going to help Shannelle. So, he could have been upstairs without the girls for at least a couple of minutes."

She asked again, "Why did you phone me, Ned?"

I closed the chocolate box. (I had eaten five. That was enough. They were meant for Timbers, when all was said and done.) "You had been told to meet a bloke, later that night. I needed to know where."

"What's this about?"

I said frankly, "The stolen cigarettes from the dockyard."

She dipped her head and frowned. "I didn't know about that."

"You were supposed to keep someone occupied. I know that much but I need the details."

"Look, Ned. There's a bloke and he's in a mess. Let me get things sorted. Give me a couple of days. You'll still get some arrests, I promise."

"I don't need his name, Timbers."

She sighed. "He asked me to go down to the yacht harbour and wait for a brown van with two windows at the front. I'd get twelve quid if I got the driver away from the cab and kept him busy for three and a half minutes. That's how long it would take to tamper with the van, my bloke said. Nothing dangerous, Ned, but enough to stop it from working." She looked me hard in the face. "You know about this, don't you? Who's telling you?"

I got to my feet. "Keep out of trouble," I said.

"Am I in trouble?"

"Not if you leave things alone."

"I can't do that, Ned. You know that I've got to find who killed him. It's taking bloody liberties murdering one of my blokes while he was still in the house. I can't let people get away with it, can I? We didn't like him but, for God's Sake, no business can go round letting their customers get murdered. We've got to show that we're on the side of the good guys. Otherwise, we'll never work again."

"I'd have thought this was good for you. A bit of scandal."

"Good for bringing on the weirdo's and bad 'uns."

"You look tired, Timbs. Let me go and you get some sleep."

She liked that idea. She said quietly, "What are the nugatory endowments of dyspeptic townsfolk?"

"Do what?"

"Stuart asked me, the other night, and I couldn't answer him. We were in the vestry and he was reading to me. He's found a bookshelf of old books and he does it every night. Reads a passage. One of the books said 'the nugatory endowments of dyspeptic townfolk.' I promised I'd ask."

"It beats me," I shrugged. "Something to do with indigestion, I guess."

Timbers was laying her head on her pillow as I left. She said, more to herself than to me, "I've hidden it in the vestry. Well, not so much hidden it as tucked it away so that no-one can find it." Her little voice reminded me of the meandering nonsense that a child gives before dropping off to sleep.

Ruby Redinutt had wandered off, so Timbers was alone when I left. She closed her eyes and promised to think of nothing until she had slept. But her peace was soon interrupted. A lady doctor, who had treated her in Casualty six hours before, put her head around the door and announced, "Nothing's broken."

Timbers welcomed her. "Come in. Come in." She sat up in bed, punched her pillows into shape, then made a space for the doctor to sit on the bedclothes.

"I can't be too long," she warned. "And you know what Matron will do if I'm caught sitting on the bed. They'll be a right to-do. But I wanted to pop in and talk to you myself —-"

'Pop in,' Timbers reflected silently. 'That sounded nice. Why can't I 'pop in' anywhere?'

" —Rather than leave it to other people."

Timbers smiled. "Anyone could have told me that I've broken no bones."

"Yes, Miss Woodcock."

"Timbers. I've told you to call me Timbers."

"I'll try," she smiled. "Did I see your boyfriend in the corridor?"

"Not on your life. He's too old and he probably farts in bed. Most men do at his age."

The Doctor laughed. "You ought to come and see us more often, Miss Woodcock. You perk the place up."

"Your Matron wants me to visit the scab clinic," Timbers moaned.

"Well, well, Matron might find that we are a couple of steps ahead of her."

Timbers' face froze. "My God, don't tell me."

"No, no. There are no infections, although you have been badly beaten up down there."

"I need to tell you about that, one day."

"Yes, but there's something else we need to talk about, isn't there?"

Timbers felt a lump swell in her throat, and the tops of her podgy cheeks blushed. "I am, definitely, then?"

"Definitely."

"I had thought, wondered, possibly. Well, I've known. I've not told anybody. I've not really spoken to myself about it. Not properly. But, I am, properly?"

"Oh yes, Timberdick. Properly or improperly, you're pregnant."

FIVE

Piggy Tucker's Fancies

Timberdick deserved a fate sweeter than murder. What good would a knife in the neck do – even if simple 'Piggy' Mo Tucker could conjure up the wickedness to stick it in? No, Timbers deserved to suffer for years knowing that dumpy Piggy was licking her lips, every minute. Good, if Timbers saw it coming but could do nothing about it. Better still, if it was her own fault. Retribution of her own making. "Oh sweet justice. Justice indeed," Piggy Tucker said to the mirror.

She was sitting on the chair, the wrong way round, and leaning over its back as she studied her sow's chin in the dressing table mirror and tried to pluck the black whisker – like wire, it was – from her mole. Piggy was as white as talcum powder and wearing only a pink see-through nightdress. It had pink frills gathered around its low neck and down its baggy sleeves. She couldn't keep it on her broad shoulders – she had tried flapping her arms and tugging and pulling, but the Bri-Nylon kept falling down.

Because the chair was back to front and Piggy had to sit awkwardly, with one knee either side of the back, the nightie had ridden up to her waist. (She loved showing off her dimpled bottom, did our Piggy. When no-one else was in the room, of course.) What with the bottom of the nightie tucked up and the top slipping down, it was hardly worth wearing. But Piggy wanted to look pretty in front of the mirror.

Ouch! The whisker wouldn't come. Damn! She got cross, now fighting with the nightdress. "Poo!" She tensed her tummy, leant forward, just a little more, and broke wind. "Oh my!" she laughed, because no-one would dream of Piggy doing that. (She did lots of things on her own. She called them Tucker's Naughties.)

It would have to be something that Ned understood, she thought, returning to the matter of Timbers' just deserts. The difficulty – the real difficulty – was that Piggy would never be clever enough to trap the little tart. Timbers was a snappy alert terrier while Piggy was a blubbery porker, ponderous with slobbery jaws and easily hurt. She pictured them as two Disney characters and went 'flubber-flubber-flubber' in the mirror.

Then the joke disappeared. The clock in the living room struck twelve, the news came on the radio and she realised how late I was.

"You hurt me on purpose," she said bitterly and turned away from the mirror so that she wouldn't see the jealousy smart in her eyes. "You're with her, Ned. And you know that I know. And — " Ooh, how she wanted to hurt someone. "Blah!" Then she tossed the chair aside and jogged from the bedroom to the kitchen. "I want to be good," she said out loud between sniffs and sucking through her mouth. "I've promised not to be bad and I've said that if you let me stay, — " from the kitchen to the bedroom and out to the hall again, " — I won't go on about things. I won't get cross and I won't blubber. I won't do anything bad." She went to the lavatory but couldn't do anything because she couldn't sit still. She was crying properly now. "And if you can tell that I've been crying, you'll throw me out. And, God, how I want to be good." She came out of the bathroom, holding the hem of her nightdress up to her waist so that she could run freely from room to room. "It's her! She's got to be there. All the time. 'Being things' to people." Piggy made a face as she mocked men's reaction. "Oh, Timberdick, you sexy thing. Oh, Timberdick, you slovenly girl. Oh, Timberdick, you cheeky scamp! Oh Timberdick – always ready. Never going away. Never – never, ever out of it."

Ten minutes later, she was cried out and sitting on the hearthrug with her knees up. "I want to be good, Ned." (She was still alone in the flat. At twenty past twelve, I was tethering my bicycle beneath the concrete arches.) "I want to be good but she calls me names like Lav-Lady or Toilet Brush and every minute you spend with her, she's making you think of me in the same way." Then she wiped her nose on the back of her arm, sucked, and promised to get better. "Straighten yourself out, Tucker. Get tough, girl. Get cheeky."

* * *

On a cold night in 1962 – the Tuesday between Marilyn Monroe's death and the barring of Ned Machray from the Police Club for the last time – I found Piggy Tucker sitting on a mossy milestone, half way up Old Moore's Lane. She had one sandal off and, with one leg crossed over the other, she was picking grit from the ball of her foot. The milestone said E.F.D. 16. In the olden days, Moore's was a cart track that ended at an old oak jetty and the carriers charged a rate per mile for hauling cargo to the larger and richer East Fairey Dock. Now, Moore's Lane got no further than the greyhound stadium fence. Piggy cleaned lavatories there, four nights a week.

"Jack won't let me in," she said. "He says he's sick of women sitting in his cafe in the middle of the night."

I put my cloak around her shoulders. "Come on. I'll get some soup and you can drink it in his back room. I'll see that he lets you."

She was always a lonely woman with little to do and nowhere to go. She became one of the characters that I'd keep an eye out for during my nightshifts on Goodladies Road. Girls, like Black Layna, Timberdick and Betty 'Slowly' Barnes. Jack in his all night café. And Dave the Taxi Man; he used to park down at the ferries, get out of his car and sit on the ropes of the little fishing boats on the slipway. A lad called Sean on the late night ferries used to play an old Fender guitar. I remember him sitting on his window ledge one night, his legs out on the brickwork as he played Hank Marvin's Midnight to the folk in the street. Then there were the people that no-one liked. Like, Gordon Freya in the early 50's and Bugger McKinley who had cheated more money out of more people on Goodladies Road than anyone else. And a lonely chap called Berkeley. 'I hate women,' he used to tell anyone who would listen. 'I've not worked for fifteen years and I'm not working now.'

These figures peopled the night, coloured it and gave it a feeling. They seemed to blend into the picture of wet cobblestones, mist around orange street lamps and the sounds of life behind frosted pub windows. People say that I had a pastoral approach to policing my beat, but it had taken me years to learn it.

During the war, I had an obscure job that sent me to the Suffolk-

53

Cambridgeshire border and, one night, to a parish hall where the local people were staging a revue. The village schoolteacher dressed up as a cockney barmaid and delivered the 'he do policemen in different voices' bit. I wasn't a great poetry man and I had never read The Wasteland but, while her performance did not encourage me to read T S Elliot, it did make me want to meet his characters. So, when I returned to police work in the 1950's I began to look at folk in a different way. I began with people around the dockyard gates and in the greyhound stadium and at speedway, and the children playing in the street after tea. I soon developed a strong personal image of the people I was serving. If I had been any good at it, I would have painted them as matchstick men coming out of factories or going to football games.

But I knew that looking and listening wasn't enough. I was collecting people – capturing them, if you like – but I still didn't know them. I had first seen Timberdick in 1958 – she was sleeping in the porch of St Mary's Church – but it was another five years before I visited her flat and talked to her properly and spent a night in the police station looking into her background.

I was her policeman and her friend. People said that we were something more, but falling in love with Timberdick was a challenge I never quite managed. I ended up knowing Betty 'Slowly' Barnes the longest. Slowly and I were friends for over fifty years.

I never liked Piggy Mo Tucker. She told fibs. That was Tucker's trouble. Mind, her face always told me when she was fibbing and that meant I could trust her. I asked her to look after my flat when I was exiled to the country patches in 1964. (She had been sleeping in the kennel block at the greyhound stadium, so staying at my place was very comfortable.) I asked Sean to keep an eye on her.

The morning after the murder, I got home from the hospital, tired and worried, and didn't want to find her, sitting plump and round shouldered on my sofa. I didn't want to listen to her, but she started, of course.

"It's like being at school," she said. "You, me and Timberdick are friends but you're always showing me that Timberdick's your best friend. Where's the place for me, Ned? Walking behind? Is that it? Always trying to catch you up. I don't want us to be lovers, Ned. I mean, I know we never will so where's the point in wanting it? And you've got your Sergeant's wife. I know that she does things with you that no-one else could do the same." (Lord, why did she have to mention that? I mean, it had nothing to do with the Stew-house Murder.) "But I want to be your special friend," she was saying. "The one you share secrets with." A sorry tear trickled down the side of her cheek and over her bull nose. Crying always made Piggy Tucker look even more out of shape. "But I'm not." She said, "I mean, I'm not, am I?"

"You followed her to the Curiosity Shop, didn't you?" I asked. I was in the kitchen with the back door open so that I could hang my cycling cape on the balcony to air.

"Not really," she replied quickly.

But I didn't believe her. I marched into the living room and accused her. "You were spying on her again, Piggy Tucker." (I only called her 'Piggy' to her face when I was cross. Usually I said 'Mo'.)

"No. No, I wasn't." She sniffed. She was crying now without any tears. "I wasn't," she pleaded like a child to a cross dinner lady. "I promised I wouldn't. It was Aunt Em, I was looking for. Sometimes she visits, you know that. I like her, Ned. I've said that I'm going to be like her one day. I've told you, that's what I want. So, it's easy for me to talk with her, that's what it's about, Ned. Ned, I'm going to buy a man's cigarette holder so that I can smoke through it like she does. I'm going to buy it tomorrow, Ned, straightaway."

I collected my own briar and my at-home tobacco pouch from the mantelpiece and stood on the hearthrug as I put the two together. "Tell me everything you saw, Mo."

She was worried. She said, "You're going to punish me."

"Oh, for God's Sake, don't be stupid!"

"All the times I've deserved it and you've never done it. I've been waiting for you to and you never have. Now I've done nothing wrong and you're going to punish me."

I shouted at her. "I won't put up with your stupidness, Piggy!"

That made her cry. Well, she wanted to. But she was back to snivelling quietly in less than a minute.

"I will," she said. "I will tell you. I do want to be good, Neddie."

Neddie! I can't stand that. It's only one better than Edwin. I had told her off about it before, but sometimes Piggy liked to aggravate. I said nothing. I had got my pipe going and waited for the smoke to clear from around my head before nodding for her to continue.

"I wanted to see who was visiting Timbers. I just wanted to know, that's all."

"You wanted to know if I was calling on her?"

"No, Ned. Really, no. I just wanted to know who. So I stayed in the alley and watched."

"You saw the dead man arrive."

She nodded. "And before that Mr Crosby and the man who pretends to be his brother – they didn't go in but they thought about it. And David Barton –Aunt Em's little boy."

"David's not a little boy," I corrected. So much of what Piggy said was laced with nastiness. What was this 'pretends to be his brother'? What did she mean? I was certain that she knew no secrets about the Crosby family. She was being mischievous. "David must be thirty, at least."

"He still lives at home, though."

"He doesn't," I argued. "He taken a room with the butcher. Now, just tell me the truth, Mo."

"Well, he was there before anyone. And he must have been with Layna, because Timbers and Shannelle came out to check the supper in the coalhouse." She saw that I was puzzled. "The supper for the ghost," she explained. "Widow McKinley says it has to be left every night."

I was so irritable that I had smoked a pipe of tobacco in only a few minutes. I looked around for the pouch. "Who did you see leave the house?"

"No-one," she stated, very quickly.

"Gordon Freya was there. Or thereabout. Did you see him come or go?"

"Oh no," she said. But the tell-tale redness appeared around her ears.

"Piggy Tucker, did you go to the stew-house to meet Gordon Freya, that night?"

"No! And you can't say that! You don't know anything and you're just guessing. You don't know anything, Ned Machray. You're just horrible!"

Tuesday was Timberdick's favourite type of day. At two in the afternoon, the sun came out after a good shower of rain and, as she knelt by Bugger's grave, the ground felt fresh and cold and brightly coloured. She pulled some weeds from the bed, then patted the turf flat and moved her knees to a cleaner patch of grass. The caretaker, John Stamp, was making noises as he sorted out his shed, twenty yards away. And the youth on probation was pushing a mechanical mower along the new graves, down by the gate. Birds were singing now that the rain had gone and there was enough water on the road to make light swishing sounds as the cars went past. Timbers felt like singing rock 'n' roll.

Aunt Em came walking up the cemetery path. Pastels in chiffon, ribbons in twists, and buttons where they had no place to be, Emily Barton (nee Sweatman) was fighting her age. She had the look of a woman who had been fighting for years but, like all worthy warriors, had no way of knowing when the battle was lost. She crowed. She gushed. She waved her painted fingernails (showing the wrinkled backs of her hands at the same time). She mouthed 'my dear' and 'how awful' in ways that used to make her eyes sparkle. She knew that they didn't now; they watered and, at the wrong time of day, took on a jaundiced look. 'I want to be joyful,' she said to the woman in the mirror each morning. 'I've always been joyful.' Then, 'Aspirate, my dear. Aspirate to show breathless mystery.'

Before the war had been her best time. Now she even accentuated being out of date so that you might think she was from the Edwardian world rather than the back streets of a city in the depression. She had been twenty in the thirties and felt no need to follow the 'quite awful' fashions of today. She would have been pleased if people thought she had been part of a set. Sometimes, she pretended that they did, because she wanted to be that sort of woman. (But her crowd had never been smart enough to be called a set. They were commonly seen on the waiting benches outside the old police court.)

"I saw you from the gate," she explained when she reached Bugger's grave. The man's cigarette holder wobbled between her teeth as she spoke. She wasn't smoking it. "I'd have walked on if I hadn't. I didn't have time for the old sod when he was alive, so why should I now? That's what I say. But I wanted to thank you. My stupid son was upstairs when the murder was done and you looked after him"

Timbers went on tidying.

"Maggie said you would do the right thing. She stayed with me overnight and wants to go back today, but I'm not sure. I'll take her to the Hoboken tomorrow and see how things go. She's still not sure what happened."

"She told the police that we didn't kill him," Timbers said.

"Because she knows you didn't. She says it was Bugger's ghost who did it."

"Bugger's dead," said Timbers. "He can't murder anyone."

"She wants people to believe he did."

"What else did she say?"

"She knows about you," Aunt Em said.

Timbers kept her face down. Em wasn't talking about the murder now. She was being nosy. "Nobody knows," Timbers said.

"Everyone who matters does and we want to know what you're going to do."

"You want to gossip, Emily Barton. You want to tittle-tattle about me."

"No dear, we don't need to gossip about your baby. A woman needs people around her in these circumstances."

"Circumstances? Is that what it is? A circumstance?"

"Timberdick, my dear, we're here. The three of us, Barbara Bellamy, Maggie McKinley and I. Maybe we can help. Put you in touch with people, perhaps."

Timbers searched the woman's face. "I don't need that kind of help. Not this time."

"Then a few kind words at the right time."

"What are you? Three witches with all the answers?"

Aunt Em tossed her head. "We should have the answers with so many years between us. You need to decide if our answers are right."

Timbers straightened her back so that she was sitting on her heels at the graveside. "Well, I'm afraid Timberdick Woodcock knows nothing about right or wrong answers. Life's given me bloody little to go on. I didn't know my father. I had a Nan until I was fifteen. When she died, I ran away from home and waited for my mum to find me. She never came looking. The lady doctor says that mum didn't know how to love." Timbers put her hand to her forehead. "That's what they say about tarts, Em. We do it because no-one taught us how to love properly. Is that it? I'm scared that I'm going to be no better for my baby. I don't think I've got anything better to give. Nothing better than what my mum gave me. I don't know what makes a special moment for a kid. I never had any. I don't know what makes the sun shine when it rains."

Emily was at a loss to respond. "Talk to Ned," she said.

Timbers laughed. "Does Ned know that I'm pregnant?"

"I told him." She waited for Timbers' reaction. "And I can't keep standing like this, so I'm going to find a seat."

Later, when Timbers joined her on the park bench, Em commented, "Do you tend the grave each week?"

"Mostly. Widow Mack can't get down here as often as she'd like. Sometimes, I bring her with me and she sits on this bench and grumbles at him while I tidy up the grass and flowers."

"People tell stories about you and old Ted."

This time, Timbers allowed the woman's nosiness. "You mean, he used to do me up the bum?" The quiet was disrupted by Mr Stamp's effort, putting the mower in the shed. "It's right. The first time, I was 16. And every week until I was twenty, while Mrs McKinley was playing whist at the Hoboken, he'd lay me face down on his bed, have a good look, then get on with it. It got so that it hurt me so much that I said he couldn't do it anymore. And he said, fine; he didn't argue. He said, can you do me a peep show, then? And for years and years he'd sit in the chair with the room half dark and I'd walk around taking my clothes off. He always wanted me to talk about ordinary things while I was doing it. Shopping, people next door, things in the street. He never asked me to touch him. Then it got as we were doing it once or twice a year. You know the last time, he fell asleep. There I was showing him my liquorice allsorts like sweets in a shop window and he dropped off. He never did see my arse again, poor bugger. I'd go round and see him of course and Mrs

59

Mack knew what it was all about but she said that seeing it again would do him no good. Sad really. Most men are sad."

"You can't sleep in the vestry if you're pregnant. Neither, the brothel beneath the old woman's bedroom. You'll have to go back to your flat. I've had a quiet word with your landlady."

Timbers let the butterflies settle on the garden leaves. "So. She's admitting she was wrong, is she? She shouldn't have thrown me out?"

"She's forgiven you."

"That's not the same," Timbers said stubbornly. "I'm not going back."

"Well, do you know who the father is, at least?"

"I'm still choosing," she said.

"The man with the walking stick would have suited. We always said he had money."

"You knew him?"

"One or two of us would have recognised him. He was round here for a couple of weeks in '52 or '53. Mind, he didn't have his stick then. He took an interest in Gordon Freya. He helped Gordon draw his bare ladies. But no-one knew his name. Your Ned might remember him."

"Ned's not mine."

Aunt Em suggested, "What about the new Detective Sergeant. He'd make a good father."

Timbers stuck out her bottom lip. "No, there's something of a lie about him. He presents himself like a television actor – a bit rugged but decent, straightforward. You'd expect him to do the right thing – like not pushing for my alibi so that I could leave the kid out of it. But when I said, do you want to see my breasts, he said yes. Now a man, a straightforward type of person would have said no. Now, Ned Machray, he wouldn't have said yes."

"So, Ned for the father. He's just right."

"Too old, of course. No, the Dad's got to be thirty-four-ish."

"The new Curate then? He cares for you. He came for tea and said we should get you back home."

Timbers smirked ungraciously. "Courting the Curate, are you?"

"I used to do the flowers," said Emily. "I still like to know what goes on in St Mary's."

"That's why everyone calls you 'Aunt Em'." But Timbers was shaking her head. "The Curate's unreliable. He let me have the key to the vestry. I mean, you can't count on a man as trusting as that, can you? Not where a child's concerned. And he offered me a room in his house. Not because I'm Timberdick but because I'm anyone. I mean, that's no good is it? A man's got to show some judgement. Besides, he'd probably want to marry me. You know, properly. No, I'm only looking for a father for my child, not a husband."

"Don't you think 'truth' has something to do with it?" Aunt Em asked carefully. "The child will want its real father."

"God, no. That's an awful thought. Picking a man just because you've slept with him. That's got to be the worse way of choosing a father for your child. Mums are supposed to look out for their babies, you know. And that doesn't mean trusting to nature. The trouble is, if I choose the father, I'll choose a wrong 'un."

* * *

The afternoon was hot, the kids were off school and the shopping centres buzzed with pop music, splashing water and football gossip. This was the summer of pirate radio, and tinny transistors played the Fab Forty on the counters of the small dress shops. (Here in the sticks, it would be another twelve months before people called them boutiques.) In the cobbled streets around Goodladies Road, it seemed that no-one was working. Here, the ton-up boys outside the Bluebird Café, with their leathers open because of the heat, wanted nothing to do with radios; they insisted that their jukebox played old hits by Carol Deane and Susan Maugham. People looked for shade. Mrs Manson carried her tabby cat to the concrete bench in the concrete bus shelter. With a Thermos of warm tea, she watched the world go by. Taxicabs covered with summer dust. Buses smelling of hot diesel. The clattering of long goods trains, two miles away. And, more than usual that afternoon, Navy planes in the bright sky. Mr Berkeley, the man who said that he hadn't worked for fifteen years and hated women, walked to the railway station and drank mugs of tea in the Station Master's office. "Have you seen this?" asked the railwayman. Last night's rag reported that 'Town' would start the new season with a young centre half who had the good looks and style to put their little provincial club on the covers of the fashion monthlies. 'We don't want him to do rock 'n' roll,' grumbled the old men. 'We need a youth who can chop legs.' Everywhere was a feeling that no-one should be disturbed. Whatever the folk were supposed to be doing, no-one could be bothered to do it.

When Ruby Redinutt heard in the locker room, fifteen minutes past the end of her shift, that the girls were gathering outside Sean's record shop, she decided to make friends with them. She went home and changed into something not too tarty – jeans and the gingham blouse that she called her cowgirl shirt – and made her way down Goodladies Road.

Girls called Dorothy Rose Redinutt learn to be Ruby. This one was every family's sorry cousin, the serious child who won Monopoly on 28 December when everyone had lost interest in the game. Dorothy Rose's achievements often came without congratulation but the child within her was too precocious to believe that life was a cheat. She learned by listening to grown-ups. Grown-ups admired her natural curls – oh, you're so lucky – but thanked God that they didn't have to endure them. It doesn't matter that you're no good outside, they said. (They meant sports and mixing with others, but Dorothy Rose felt that she was good at nothing beyond the front door.) You must always be grateful for your curls, they kept saying, and your lovely brown eyes will break a few hearts. But then, one day, her mother said that not being pretty didn't matter either. Of course, it was a spiteful thing for a parent to say. So, when Dorothy Rose was thirteen – and already 'Rube' at school – her curly hair and brown eyes came to nothing. All she had was a heavy bust – great emerging monsters, they felt – and she didn't know what to do with it. Even now, twenty-three years old and a policewoman, she was most comfortable walking with her arms folded in front. She had joined the Police Force because she believed that she would be told to cut her hair and she'd never be out of doors in clothes she had to choose. 'Oh no,' said the Inspector. 'Just pin your hair up, dear. We can't go cutting off those lovely curls, can we?' Of course not, thought Dorothy-Rose.

I saw her as I crossed the junction. She looked better than usual, I noticed. She had brushed her hair until it took on a fly-away mode and she was wearing high-heeled boots that made her bottom stick out and her hips wiggle. I raised a hand to say hello, then pushed through the doors of the Hoboken Arms.

She wasn't sure how she was going to introduce herself. She had tried so many lines in her head but none of them sounded convincing. Then she decided to be herself, an off duty policewoman who was looking for Timberdick. She'd say … No, don't rehearse it, Rube. Just say it as it comes.

Two of the Goodladies girls were in Sean's record shop, a converted corner terrace house where Rossington Street met a paved alley. A third girl was sitting on the doorstep in sandals, no stockings and a home made miniskirt that showed her suntanned thighs. All the girls were smoking but Merle on the doorstep was making the best show of it, drawing deeply then cocking her head as she blew the smoke through lips shaped for kissing. Now and then, the girls indoors would call coarse things to her and she would answer without turning her head. The man behind the counter was fifty-two. He had no collar on his shirt and his braces were down around his waist. He was reading a newspaper, spread across an open drawer of 45's. An almost empty roll-up was stuck to his bottom lip.

"We're waiting for Sean," said the curly blonde on the windowsill.

"I've told you. He's round Ned's. They're taping the old geezer's jazz records."

"Where's his guitar then? Come on, Bradley, we could have a go on his guitar while he's not here."

By two o'clock Layna Martins had joined the girl on the doorstep. With Shannelle and a new girl from Salisbury, they formed a clutch of chattering chicks on a street corner. Now that the stew-house had closed, the girls had to find somewhere to congregate and, although no-one had suggested that the record shop should take its place and no arrangement had been made with the old buzzard, the girls knew that the house had two empty rooms upstairs. And, down the alley, was a side gate to a back yard.

The girls talked of Timberdick and her Toilet Brush, Sean and his

Telecaster and poor Baz Shipley who was up for thieving again. She'd go down this time, all the girls said.

"Berkeley's not here," said the blonde on the windowsill. "I'm worried about that. He's been following me for days and he should be here."

Ruby saw them as soon as she turned into Rossington Street. Half a dozen young women, two hundred yards ahead. One of them noticed her, even at that distance, and warned the others that a W.P.C. in civvies was coming. Two or three of the girls stepped into the gutter to look.

Make friends, Ruby reminded herself. But what did that mean? What did she want? Was it enough, this first time, that they should talk nicely to her as she walked past? Or would the afternoon be a failure if she didn't manage to stand with them, chatting. And what if they invited her inside? That would show that they liked her. And what if they had a man upstairs, waiting for a new girl to come along? She had thought about that. She knew that she wanted to do it. But she hadn't made up her mind to go ahead.

At that moment, Piggy Mo Tucker reached the girls, having walked from the other end of the paved alley.

"Here she is!" yelled the curly haired one.

"It's her fault Timbers is out on the street!"

Confused, Piggy stood in the middle of Rossington Street while the angry women clustered around her.

Ruby was still twenty yards away but saw what was going to happen. She didn't try to stop them. She heard Piggy plead, "I didn't get her thrown out."

"No, but Ned would take her in, if you weren't there."

It started with a shove. Long tall Helena thrust the heel of a hand against Piggy's shoulder. Piggy stepped back to keep her balance but was immediately pushed forward by hands from behind. Two girls threw punches into her ribs, but the assaults weren't serious at that stage.

Black Layna tried to stop it. "Come on, girls. Timbers wouldn't let you do this. Let the Toilet Brush alone."

But Layna's careless use of the nickname prompted a chorus of catcalls. Arse paper! Bog roll! Pig's bladder! There was shouting and squeals and the gang gathered pace. Layna got between them but took an elbow painfully to the belly and went backwards, crouching.

Then Helena kicked out and Piggy went to the ground. "Yeah!" the girls cheered and closed in, kicking and stamping, or reaching down to pull at their victim. They started to chant a silly clapping song that the pirate radio ships had been plugging throughout the summer. The stamping and catcalls got a nasty hysteria going. Shannelle sat on Piggy Tucker's chest, with her thighs astride the woman's throat. She pulled her hair. So hard, that she seemed determined to wrench it out and leave poor Piggy with patches.

Bradley, holding the scruff of a girl's neck in each hand, came to the corner door, threw the girls out and then locked the door and pulled down the blinds. "Bloody hell, Bradley!" they cried.

"See what you've done now!" Helena shouted, delivering another kick. "You've got our mates thrown out of the shop. Toilet Brush!"

Ruby Redinutt stayed on the opposite pavement. She didn't shout. She didn't step forward. She stood with her fingers in her mouth and watched. Layna noticed her and stood aside from the gang and stared at Ruby's mesmerized face. The policewoman, because she did nothing about the fight, had said so much.

Piggy Tucker was muttering, although no-one could hear. She'd get Timbers back, she promised. She was a bloody coward, a skinny bloody coward, for getting others to do her dirty work. New rules, she kept saying. From now on, Piggy was allowed to do whatever she wanted about Timberdick Woodcock. Nothing was unforgivable. "Timbers deserves a fate sweeter than murder," she said out loud and promised to think one up.

SIX

A Night Duty

Bedroom Number Four at the Hoboken Arms had the best acoustics that Sean could find, so he convinced Chloed – our West Country landlady – to give him the room for nothing and told me to bring along a selection of my 78's. He wanted to record some of my favourite New York jazz sides as part of a musical archive, he said. He set the tape recorder and the record player on two felt covered card tables. He caught me looking at the bodged alterations to the recorder's deck. "I bought it from Berkeley. He added a lot more facilities to bring it into sync with the record player. Or so he says. I don't really understand. Mind you, it wasn't a cheap job when he bought it, new from Kerry's, five years ago. It cost him eighty guineas, even then. I could never afford anything like it." He looked admiringly at the machine, allowing me plenty of time to be impressed. But neither of us knew anything about hi-fi; Sean wasn't a scientific or enquiring type. He was barely twenty but his fine fawn hair was already receding and he was trying to compensate by growing a beard; something that he didn't have the wherewithal to deliver. He looked arty and dippy and not at all logical. "Have you heard of Kerry's in Perivale?" I said that I hadn't. "Me neither. But Berkeley goes on about it all the time. As if it's some sort of shrine for experts."

"I doubt it. Mr Berkeley's an expert at nothing worthwhile."

"It's a Telefunken."

Yes. It said that on the machine.

"Berks did tell me the number, but I've forgotten."

"85KL," I said, reading the little gold sticker on the case.

"You can feed the music direct from the record player by this lead here, and there's a separate lead for the microphone. But we can't superimpose our voices over the music without dulling the sound, so we've got to keep the music clean and record your comments after each song."

"What about the wow and flutter?" I had heard enthusiasts talk about this in the police canteen, but Sean knew that I didn't know what it meant.

"Sounds like two of your girls, Mr Ned. Wow and Flutter. Who's that then? Timberdick's Wow. But who's Flutter these days? You've got that mad woman living with you but ask me and I'll say nothing's going on. You used to have a thing with that lady Inspector but you've always played that down."

"There was nothing to it," I said quietly.

"There's a whisper that you're carrying on with a policeman's wife. Oh, and there's a new policewoman about. What about her, Mr Ned? You like a young woman in uniform."

I said it was time we played some records.

"The word is, she was close to the murder. Practically standing outside, people say."

"The Nore Road was her beat," I said.

"Is that right? Do W.P.C.'s have beats, Mr Ned? Someone told me that they don't normally. So what was she doing there, Mr Ned?"

"Doing as she was told, I expect. The girls quite often do a walk."

"But not regularly. Not normally. Have you got a soft spot for her?"

"I've come here to play records, Sean."

"So, you're not saying yes and you're not saying no, eh?" he teased.

I said there was nothing to say. I was too old to have girlfriends and I hadn't experienced many even when I wasn't too old. He said he didn't believe me and I said my first choice of records came from California, not New York.

Sean didn't like the first two Ben Pollack sides. He said they sounded like cartoon music, especially when the Williams Sisters joined in. But when he heard Jack Teagarden delivering 'Beale Street Blues', he was as bowled over as I knew he would be. Then I gave him Wingy Manone on Red Nichols' 'Rocking Chair' and followed it with 'Corrina Corrina' by the same team. Sean was very enthusiastic because, he said, it was a Bob Dylan song. I had heard this man, Bob Dylan, and knew that he was the typical make-do American folk singer that wouldn't last twelve months. But liking Bob Dylan was 'hep' in 1965 (my word, not Sean's) because when I was ready to say that 'Corrina Corrina' was much older than Mr Dylan and would still be around when Mr Dylan was forgotten, a desperate look on Sean's face indicated that he didn't want such wisdom committed to tape. So, I kept quiet. I knew that he liked The Rolling Stones, so I concluded my record selection with the Muddy Waters track that inspired their name. Sean was well pleased, probably because the reproduction was so poor that the thing just had to be rare.

It was half past six before Sean concluded the recording session. I hadn't slept since the night duty and knew that I would have little time for a nap if I returned home. Chloed grumbled; she was running a hotel, she said, not a doss house where tramps and dodgy dealers could drop in for a couple of hours sleep. "Go on, Ned Machray, take Number Twelve at the back of the first floor. And sleep on top of the blankets, do you hear? I don't want you between the sheets."

And so, at five to seven, I lay my head in the Hoboken's coldest bedroom and promised myself two hours with my eyes closed. I had enjoyed the recording session — I truly felt that I was passing on, to youngsters like Sean, the music that I had learned to appreciate – but I was irritated by his comments about women and girlfriends. There was no-one in my life that I would want to be bothered with. The irritation was worse because 1965 was the year when Timberdick would hardly speak to me and Piggy Tucker wouldn't get from under my feet. An old copper with not a lot to do. That was all I wanted to be.

* * *

Picture a city churchyard in a cold twilight. The brickwork is smoked and eaten away, the paths are broken and the grass is so grimy that the ends are black. It's always cold here; even Stuart Morrison, the lad who always argues against dressing sensibly, carries his sweater over his arm when he comes to play football near his mother's grave.

The coldness is made eerie by the sounds of draughts moving about the high roofed nave and the stairs and the corners where things are hidden. And the creaking of the wooden beams and banisters. The cold is not because of the high walls or the tall oaks that stop the sunshine getting in, Timbers says, or the stone and concrete that soak up what warmth might otherwise have been. Timbers says it's because of the spirits.

Poor women called wicked and wanton a hundred years ago still yearn to be understood. Girls more wronged than wayward. Wives told to suffer and spinsters always suspected. Their souls still hang in the air. These are the ghosts of the real poor church mice. Timbers says. And she has thought about it a lot. For years, the men in the church had told other men it was all right to do women down.

Timbers was pregnant for the fourth time in her life, but this time she didn't fear the little one. 'Properly pregnant,' the lady doctor had said and all those questions that had been free falling in Timbers' head for several weeks – bumping into possible answers but always bumping off them – now came together. And Timbers was surprised how settled it felt. This time, she was sure of herself. She was pleased to be pregnant and, with that pleasure, so many of the questions no longer required answers. Timbers wasn't looking for 'choices', she needed no 'solutions'.

The doctor had warned her that things might be difficult. 'You've had a rough time before and you're not in good shape.'

She had been thirteen, the first time, and lost the baby near the beginning. The second and third times, she had been pregnant in the city. On the streets and on the game. A woman in Cleremont Street helped. "Oh, don't worry, she's no longer here to take the blame," she told the lady doctor. "But, the last time she warned me that another visit to her parlour would be the death of me."

The doctor had fidgeted. "God, Timbers, why can't we do things properly? Come a day when we won't have you girls scuttling around back streets to sort those matters. Girls — "

Girls like me? Timbers thought.

"Girls like you," the doctor said. "Will be able to choose."

Timbers hadn't been able to help her laughter. "Choose? So, we do come from different worlds, after all."

69

As Timbers walked up the Nore Road, she thought things out slowly. She would need to choose the father carefully, she decided. Someone the child could look up to, someone to follow – someone who owned the young citizen. That's what Timberdick had never known. Someone who owned her.

She got to the churchyard as the vicarage cat came up from the chlorifier cellar and trod into the shadows beneath the hazel bushes. Young Stuart Morrison, a leather football tucked under his arm, was waiting for her at the kissing gate. The schools were half way through their holidays but Stuart still wore his grey shorts and socks (one sock pushed down to his ankle). His shirt-tail was out of his trousers and mud was on every knee and elbow. He had two sisters who sang in pubs late at night and a father who was always just quick enough to keep out of trouble. He didn't see much of them but that didn't matter; Stuart had his football. No lad better deserved to be discovered as a working class soccer hero. He always had a ball at his feet. He was the boy who went on practising when the others had gone home. Every night, you would find him here, or on the railway rec, or behind the war memorial, kicking a scrub football or bald tennis ball against a marked target. Or practising headers or kick-ups. Much of the time, it was his way of keeping busy when he was alone.

"Can we sleep together? My dad's out all night and I can't do it, Timbers. I can't stay in bed on my own in the house, not when I know Mum should be there." He trotted alongside as Timbers crossed the uneven turf to the old door at the back of the church. "It was good in the hospital," he said. "I had something to eat in the canteen. Then I stayed in the Matron's office until the television started. She let me watch it in the children's ward with the others. There was this girl, Elizabeth; she was thirteen. Older than me. She showed me a picture of her Dad selling a tractor. That's really something, don't you think, Timbs? Being the person who put a tractor on a farm? Matron said I had to wait until Dad picked me up but she let me go when my sisters arrived."

Timbers had been living in the old vestry for two weeks and, although nothing in the place was her own, she had made the little room feel like a homely cabin. When Timbers shut herself in this room she pretended that she was a little white mouse in a shoebox in a cupboard beneath the staircase of a big house in town. 'The sort of house where Paddington Bear lived, or Wendy and The Darlings,' Stuart said. The quiet dustiness of the place, the aged colours of the old furniture and the mustiness that comes from windows never being open, made it easy to fancy that no-one else knew about the place. Timbers said that the cobwebs were there to keep the secret. And the secrecy had an Enid Blyton deliciousness. Stuart felt it too. But, like an Enid Blyton childhood, the magic was an illusion. Of course people knew she was there. Of course people were looking after her.

The wood-burning stove was a Godsend and she had learned to keep a stock of dry logs for each night. At first, the stove had been her only way of boiling water but on the fourth day her unannounced benefactor ran an extension lead from the office. Electricity and a kettle made all the difference. Then, last Sunday – the day before the Stew-house Murder – she had carelessly left a skirt that she had borrowed from Layna. It disappeared but came back cleaned and pressed, with some second-hand slips and cardies. Timbers had always assumed that the local Vicar or his Curate was looking after her but the pressing service suggested a cleaning woman or the lady who did the flowers in the church. She wondered if she should leave a thank you note, but the lady might see that as an invitation to introduce herself and Timbers didn't want that.

"What are we reading tonight?" Stuart said as he followed her in. He knelt at the small rack of leather bound books behind the door.

"You're always looking at the titles, chum. You decide."

Chum? he thought. She never called him 'chum'. Women didn't call men 'chum'. Chums were children.

"You choose, Morrie. I'm tired."

"Not Scholar Gypsies, eh," he said. "We've read nearly all of it."

Timbers switched the kettle on, then lay herself on the threadbare couch while her young friend reviewed the bookshelf. "I couldn't find out about dyspeptic townsfolk and the nugatory endowments," she confessed wearily. "Ned didn't know."

Stuart selected one of the small volumes and settled on the carpet. "Have you two made up? Shit, that's great. "

Timbers had not heard the lad use bad language before. She waited until he looked at her, then dipped her head and frowned while her eyes kept track of his. "Indeed," she said, all schoolma'amish. "Probably great. Just tell me what you've found out." She put a hand to her forehead, ready for sleep.

Stuart sat back on his heels. "Shannelle has gone to live with Mr Freya again. I heard their neighbour talking about it in the papershop and she said they got home at half past two in the morning and they've locked themselves indoors, ever since."

"Is she all right?"

"The neighbour didn't say, but it means something. It means that they are pretending to be in the house when they're not. Shannelle wasn't indoors this afternoon; she was outside the record shop. There was a huge fight in the street."

"I know, I know," she said wearily. "God, the world's against us, so what do we do? Fight against ourselves? Men are the enemy. Not Piggy bloody Toilet Brush."

"And Gordon Freya can't be Bugger McKinley's ghost," Stuart continued. "The neighbour says that he and Shannelle were in their back garden, first thing this morning, and that's when black Layna saw the ghost at the top of Cardew Street."

He pulled down his socks and scratched the backs of his legs until they were close to bleeding.

"Don't do that," said Timbers.

"What's changed, Timbers. You've started talking to me like a child. Are you practising for something?"

Timbers blushed furiously. She felt her face burn and hated herself. She didn't know what to say. More than anything, she wanted to avoid embarrassing the youngster. "This is silly. I don't usually blush like this."

"Mum used to say it happened when she'd been thinking about things. It's nothing to worry about."

Timbers brought her knees to her chest, wrapped her arms around her legs and looked at her toes as they wiggled on the cushion of the couch. "Someone asked me what it was like, being me. I said it was cold and wet and horrid, most of the time, but none of that describes it properly. Do you know what it feels like, Stuart? Being Timberdick Woodcock feels like wearing old clothes all the time.

72

Well, I'm going to change all that."

"You're coming off the game?" asked the young boy.

Timbers picked at the knuckle of her little toe. She didn't believe that she could stop working. She had been on the streets for nearly twenty years and the little bit of pavement opposite the Hoboken Arms had felt like her own since 1958. "I'm going to do it differently," she said. "I'm going to think differently."

"Be careful," he cautioned. "You're someone in people's lives and I know what it's like when you turn around and someone's gone." No further, he thought. I've said it, Timbers, but don't ask any more questions. The boy needed to distract her. "Timbers, why do they call it a stew-house?"

"Do you know what V.D. is?"

"I'm not soft," he protested indignantly. "V.D.'s V.D. It's what Poison Ivy's about. All the groups are playing it. Sean's got it on a Stones e.p."

"Well, hundreds of years ago."

"When?"

"I don't know," Timbers retorted, seeking to control her impatience. "But it was the olden days."

"You're talking to me as if I'm stupid again. What do you mean 'hundreds of years'? You mean, Victorian, Elizabethan, Roman or what?"

"When Shakespeare was alive. That's how someone explained it to me. I'm not brainy, Stuart."

"The Tudors, then. Carry on."

"People used to think that stewed prunes would protect blokes against V.D. so the whorehouses used to offer their punters dishes of them. Then they started to put stewed prunes in the window so that people would know what was inside."

"Like a barber's pole."

"Yes."

"Who told you that?"

"Someone."

He gave his legs one last scratch, then said, "I could help you solve the Stew-house Murder."

"You know who killed the Walking Stick Man?"

73

"No. But I know what the important clue is." When Timbers went on looking without a word, he added, "There's one condition."

"Condition? What condition? I don't let blokes set conditions, you know that."

"I saved your life."

That made her laugh.

"I did," he insisted. "Last year when all those lads were throwing stones at you, I said you could come back to my house for tea. I did, didn't I?"

"And that saved my life?"

"It's the same sort of thing," he argued.

"All right, Clever Dick. What's the clue?"

"I can't say. Not until you've heard the condition."

"No."

He shrugged. "Fine."

"Listen, you can tell me, do you hear?"

"No."

"Stuart!"

"The condition is – you date my dad. Properly, like boyfriend and girlfriend. Just once, and if you don't like each other," he shrugged again, "fine."

"Date?"

"Pictures or a dance or, I don't know, something in a restaurant. Crikey, Timbers, how would I know what you do? You can't just do men up against the walls. You must 'date' them as well sometimes."

Timbers couldn't argue. She didn't want to say that, for years, it had seemed that she only did blokes 'up against the walls'. Even when some of them, the good men that she took into her flat, did nice things like reciting poetry when she disrobed and never touched her but only wanted to talk, even then, it seemed like doing it up against the walls. Cleanly, but still the same.

"It's a deal," she said.

"Promise? I'll give you my idea and you'll take dad on a date."

"I said, it's a deal, didn't I?"

"Promise, though."

"Don't push your luck."

"All right. I'll trust you, Timberdick. Now then, I've been listening

74

to things that you have said and Uncle Ned has said, and things that those two policemen were saying on the night of the murder. "

"Yes, yes."

"And it's obvious. The thing that's missing from everyone's story is the walking stick. No-one knows where it is."

"And? So what?"

"I don't know. I never said I knew the answer, only the clue."

He started to scratch again and she told him off.

"I've only started doing it since my mum died; I never used to scratch. Now, I scratch the backs of my legs all the time."

Timberdick smiled. "Don't worry about it, Stuart. It's because you're playing football in the graveyard. The grass there's filthy. Have you noticed that the tips are all black?"

The boy's eyes filled with tears. Timbers reached for his hand and held it securely.

"Come on, kid," she said encouragingly.

"I need someone to talk to me like that. To explain things like dirty grass and other things. I've no-one since Mum's gone. Dad's all right and he tries, but Dads don't think in the same way."

Later, when she had her eyes closed and Stuart was staying awake, Timbers said, "You're Ned's grass, aren't you. You're the one he's getting his information from. That's why he phoned me on the night of the murder. Because you'd told him that I was meant to help your Dad. Stuart, you mustn't."

"I had to."

"No you didn't." But she understood his dilemma "Your Dad was involved, wasn't he? He's the one putting the job together and you wanted to stop him somehow. So you told Ned enough to bugger it up. Stuart, that's very dangerous. Lord knows what Ned thinks he's up to, using you in that way. But you're to stop. Understand me?"

"Yes Timbers."

"And thank you for the walking stick clue. I'm sure it's important."

He had so little to give her. "The job's going ahead on Friday night. I've heard Dad talking. You've got to mess things up for him, please Timbers."

* * *

I wandered through the back doors of Central Police Station at nine twenty-five, giving myself time for a cup of tea and a bun before the parade. A couple of dog handlers were there; they had been called in to patrol the scrublands along the east shore. I guessed that Bernie Trent had commissioned them. He hadn't mentioned it to me. I was knobbing some butter onto the last mouthful of teacake when Sergeant Henderson joined me. His wife didn't like him doing nights, he said. She worried when he left her alone in the house. I knew that they had recently bought an end of terrace in Osmington Street. (Henderson was one of the first Federation ranks to own his own place in the city. He had argued long and hard to get the ACC's permission.) I said I would keep an eye on the place during the shift. He told me that she would be sitting in the kitchen if she were awake. I would be able to see the light from the dustbin alley.

At nine forty, twelve policemen assembled around the long table in the locker room and listened to 'Dickie' Henderson's reading of the messages. Notes written by the front office during the previous two shifts. 'Hand-over' slips from the collator's office. And one or two 'instructions for guidance' from the Superintendent. A couple of the youngsters toadied the Sergeant by contributing to his collection of cigarette coupons. We were half way through the year and three P.C.'s had not taken their allowance of sick leave. "You, Gerry, add Wednesday to your rest days," Dickie instructed. Then he looked at me; I had already mentioned that I needed to speak about our Personal Radios. "The new twin-packs don't work round the back of Goodladies," I said. "I need to do 'points' instead." I expected him to grumble, but he conceded without a fuss. We agreed that I would phone in from Cardrew Street on the half hour and the London Road crossroads and the Nore Road junction on the alternate hours. As we detailed the arrangements the youngsters began to quietly rehearse Dixon of Dock Green's theme. Soon, the rest of the lads joined in the Mickey-taking and Dickie Henderson's parade disintegrated into laughter and table slapping.

While the shift collected batteries for their radios and traded banter, I slipped quietly out to the station yard. I took the bicycle from the railings and pedalled into the night. The grey streets were unusually quiet for a summer evening. Lovers were indoors, no doubt. Children were in front of the tele. But, as I passed the Hoboken Arms, I heard the small group of regulars singing and shouting around the posh Edwardian piano. Fed up but always rudely sexy, Shannelle was standing on Timbers' 'little bit of pavement' opposite the pub. She wanted to show off her new camel coloured boots and her tan mock leather miniskirt but it was too quiet to hope for any business. Few cars were on the roads. Shannelle was leaning against the drainpipe outside Number 143's front door and looking sullen. Her new hairstyle made looking sullen easy. When she saw me, she turned aside so that the rear of her clinging miniskirt rode up to show a little more than just the tops of her legs. Her expression didn't change – she couldn't have cared less, it said. But I knew that Shannelle dressed carefully so that no trick of exposure, no little glimpse of a cheeky treat was an accident. But where were the blokes?

As I crossed the junction, I told her to 'get along on'. She cheered up and said it was good to see me in the city again. 'Old Ned,' she called me. "Have you seen her? She said she'd be here at half past nine and it's gone ten."

"Timbers?"

"Layna."

I was trying to manoeuvre the bicycle from the road to the kerb. When things began to wobble, I stuck out a Doc Marten and pressed a hand down on my policeman's hat. I had purloined a string of sausages from the station's canteen and was carrying it, wrapped in only a brown paper bag, beneath the helmet. As I tried to keep it on, I was aware of the commotion in the pub behind me and Murphy's Law suggested that if my hat fell off or if the sausages tailed behind me like a fanciful picture of Tom Tom the Piper's Son, someone would be at the staircase window to spot me.

Without speaking of Timberdick or Layna, I waved uncertainly to Shannelle and gathered speed along the uneven pavements of the side street. Across the way, a couple were kissing madly in a porch. As I turned my head to watch, the woman opened her eyes and, just for a moment, we were looking directly at each other. She was all right. She wanted to be there. When I dismounted at the end of the street and looked back to the junction, I saw Shannelle getting into a white 1100. She looked confident, in charge and on top of her trade.

I dawdled on, reaching 'Dickie' Henderson's place a few minutes later. His wife opened her back door and said, "I wanted you to come. We've got to talk."

"I've brought the sausages," I said.

"Yes. Of course you have, but we've got to talk."

"Before or after the sausages?"

She saw that my flippancy had to be satisfied. "Oh, after, I'm sure. The sausages are what you have come for."

It was a game we played. Ruthie fried sausages, pricking and prodding them in the pan while she pretended that she was sticking the fork into other sausage-like things. She found the fantasy especially ticklish if she wore nothing but a skimpy white apron. She would never do things like this when her husband was in the room. Sometimes she did it in her head and didn't tell him, I suspect, but she liked it best of all when I was in the room to watch.

That evening, Ruthie kept her clothes on. She didn't want to chat and she didn't flirt as she usually did. Usually, Ruthie's hips would be hool-a-hooping as she sang about beef chipolatas and what she was going to do with them. Tonight, it was all a bit dry-faced. She was quiet and fed up. Obviously, something was wrong. Nothing to do with me, mind. I told myself, women are funny things. Sometimes, you just have to wait for them to tell you what's up. It's usually something trivial.

"Timberdick's pregnant," I said.

"How do you know?"

"Aunt Em guessed it weeks ago. She can, you know. Her and Widow McKinley are like a couple of witches. I didn't take any notice when she told me, but W.P.C. Redinutt heard it mentioned at the hospital. So, now, it's true. I'm not the father but I'll expect she'll ask me to be. I've always been the one she's trusted. I know we fell out last year. That was because I contacted her mother and it didn't work out. She'll come round. Oh, she'll think of others. John Peacock, perhaps. He's new to the police station and rather smart to look at. Suave, she might think, at first sight. But she'll see him as a fool before long. And she'll have taken many well-heeled chaps to her bed—bound to have done and any one of them could give her a comfortable life. The young curate at St Mary's; he's a rival. Yes, I can see that. He's tried to save her more than once. I've spotted him waiting for her at the kissing gate but she'll settle on me, not him. I'm no bother, you see, Ruthie. I won't crowd her. She'll want someone who can offer the child some wisdom. But she won't want a husband (and that's where the others will get it wrong, you see); she just wants someone to act like a father for the child."

Ruthie wasn't talking to me. She was facing the window above the kitchen sink, a view that filled most of her life these days.

"It felt good this afternoon, teaching young Sean all about jazz. It was good, 'passing it on' and that's how Timbers will want it with her child. You know, I've always felt close to her. I first met her in '58 when she was sleeping rough in the porch of St Mary's Church and even on that first meeting, I thought — "

"The baby's yours," she said sharply. She was standing at her sink, draining fat from a frying pan before delivering the sausages to my plate. I was sitting at the kitchen table, watching the freckles on her shoulders displayed by her cheap sleeveless print dress. I said that I couldn't be the father because Timbers and I hadn't slept together since the autumn.

"Not that baby," she said. "I mean, your baby. My baby. Our baby."

The world went cold and her words came through with a dullness, as if water had got into my ears. "Grief, you're having a baby."

"And there's no-one else, Ned Machray, before you say anything dreadful."

"You're pregnant?" I asked. Just wanting to be sure, that's all.

"That's how women usually have babies. You've got me pregnant, Ned, you bastard." She plonked the plate of sausages in front of me and sat at the opposite side of the table. She studied my face, then pushed the red and brown sauces towards me. "I can't leave, Dickie," she said.

"Of course not."

"There's no 'of course' about it, Ned. Leaving Dickie and bringing up my child with you ought to be one of the ideas you want to talk about."

"But I know you can't."

She looked quite attractive, in an oldish sort of way. Her rust coloured hair falling gently over her frown.

"Have you had any other children?" she asked.

"I had a son during the war, but we've lost touch. I suppose a little girl would be quite nice."

"I'll see what I can do," she said, her voice only half full of sarcasm.

I asked, " Will Dickie need to know?"

"I live with him, for God's sake!" she snapped. "Of course, he'll notice. What do you want me to do? Wear loose dresses until Christmas, then pop to the outside toilet and come back with a miracle?"

"He'll know it's not him?"

She nodded regretfully, "We've not done anything together for two years. Christ, your bloody brat won't be off my hands until I'm sixty. Christ, Ned, that's the rest of my life spoken for."

I saw the tears come to her eyes. I reached a hand across the table. "Look, Ruthie. It'll be all right. We'll be all right, the two of us. The three of us, I mean. We'll go away together, never mind Dickie."

She snatched her hand away. "God, that's awful. It's all lies, Ned. You know it is. You want Timbers' child, that's the truth, Ned. You'd rather have a bun in her oven, not mine."

"That's not true," I protested.

"Oh Ned, you should have listened to yourself, just five minutes ago. I was frying sausages, wasn't I? Preparing to give myself up to you – not for the first time, not for the twentieth – but you were picturing her, not me."

"That's not true."

"You were talking about her child and how you wanted her to say that you were the father. God, you should have heard yourself."

"That's not true. You're wrong, darling."

"Don't! Never call me darling. I am the mother of your child and nothing more. Do you understand?" She stood up and went back to the kitchen window. "So, you already have a son?"

"And there was Betty Clarke, but that was before the war. I used to drive lorries between Eastleigh and St Albans and sometimes I would stay overnight at Mrs Clarke's house. One day, she wouldn't let me in. She said her daughter was carrying my baby and I wouldn't see either of them again. I don't know what became of them. The child, my eldest child, would be more than thirty now. Perhaps I'm a grandfather."

"So you have two children?"

"Three if you count Doris Houghton's boy. And if you include my thing with Doris, then you must count Hattie Jones and Gloria Staines. The circumstances were pretty much the same. All boys. I really would like a girl."

"So how many children do you have?"

I sighed. "Does any man know for sure?"

"Then just the ones you know about."

I hesitated. I mouthed the word. Then croaked it, and she told me to speak up.

"Eight."

"Oh, eight," she teased. "Quite a dormitory, Mr Machray. And not one of the women mean anything to you."

"You do," I said promptly, but she knew that I was lying. "Really, hen, I want us to go away somewhere and bring up our baby in a family."

"Shut up! Oh God, shut up. Your falseness just makes things worse. I'll have your baby and you'll spend time with him – with her, if I can promise you that – but always remember that you make me feel dirty. You make me feel like a dirty woman!"

The rain had started at midnight and Ruthie pushed me out when it was at its worst. I pushed my bicycle along the twitchel by the railway line and stopped for a pipe beneath some overhanging branches. I meant to get my head around Ruthie's bad news but easily found things to distract me. Although a policeman's uniform provides much protection in wet weather, you need to be aware of its failings. The cloak stops short of your knees so your trouser legs get soaked unless you cross your hands over your belly. This pushes a skirt out at the front increasing the overhang. Secondly – and importantly – you need to keep the helmet balanced forward. The wet naturally gathers at the front peak rather than on the back rim and this can produce a drip-drip-drip onto your nose. So, keep the hat forward so that the drips miss.

When the rain eased, I pushed on towards Goodladies Junction, checking the lock-up shops and the side alleys. I got as far as Rossington before I realised that I hadn't phoned in since I had left the police station. I had an excuse during the first half of the shift because the Sergeant knew that I was close to his house. After all, I was keeping an eye on his wife, but now that she was asleep, alone in her bed, he would expect me to be at the appointed telephone kiosks at thirty-minute intervals. I decided to cut along the cinder track at the side of the Secondary Modern School and call from Goodladies Junction. As I passed the stone porch of the old Methodist Rooms, I felt for my pipe in my jacket pocket, but I hadn't time to stop. Twenty yards further on, I saw that the rickety door of Smithers Motor Garage had been disturbed. The dilapidated workshop hadn't been occupied for eighteen months and I thought, maybe, that one of our vagrants had bedded down inside. I left the bike against the old brick wall and, taking the heavy torch in my hand, pushed my way into the garage.

Layna Martins was sitting in the corner of the floor with her knees up and her head to one side. She had the old fashioned dress that Timbers had made her wear on the night of the killing. She had folded it into a neat ball and was holding it to her face so that she could cry into it. (I remembered how I had found Layna in this same place, two years before. She had been horribly hurt and unable to speak. Oh, God, I thought, please not again.) This time, I sat down beside her. My fatness made it easy for her to fall against me.

"I keep seeing it, Ned," she wept. "Blood up the walls. I can feel it on my hands and in my mouth. I can't get it out of my mouth, Ned."

I made a big fuss of taking off my cycle cape and draping it across her shoulders. Blood wasn't in her mouth, I assured her, and anyway she was safe now.

She spoke with her fingers in her mouth. "His neck was open and there was some thin sort of lining that hadn't quite come free."

"No more talking," I said. "You and I, let's close our eyes and go to sleep."

"I thought Timbers was going to make me break it properly. I thought she was going to say 'Tear the lining away, Layna' because

82

she was horrible to me, Mr Ned. She made me go through the dead man's pockets."

The sound of moving concrete made us sit up. Someone was taking the slabs away from the wooden doors. The barn doors opened and a tall uniformed figure appeared from the darkness.

"How dare you!"

I recognised Sergeant Henderson's voice.

"Skip, I can explain."

"All that guff about wanting to use the police telephone boxes instead of radios. All that — " he spluttered, searching for a new word but, in his frustration, he couldn't find one. "Guff! Saying that you'll keep an eye on Ruth for me. And all the time you — you were, you were — "

"Listen, Richard, I can explain all this."

"I don't care that you're cuddling your damned tart. Good Lord, the whole station knows what you get up to, given half the chance. But when you take my trust and ... and ..."

"It's not what you think. I don't know how much you've heard but..."

"I've heard it all. I – I was sitting there in the canteen listening to it. The whole police station was listening to it!"

Surely not. I began, "Ruth's very..."

"You don't know how Ruth is! You've been nowhere near her all night. I asked you, Ned. I asked you to go round and keep an eye on her. And then, what do I hear? I hear — I hear—"

"Things need sorting out, a little."

"I hear you on a bloody pirate radio ship! There, on the wireless, in the canteen, for everyone to hear. Playing your damned jazz records when you should have been on night duty."

"That can't be so," I said, more puzzled than ever.

"No wonder, I haven't been able to track you down. Of course, you haven't kept any of your points. You've been playing at damn-fool disc jockeys"

"Skip, you must be mistaken."

"I heard it!" he shouted. "I heard it, not two hours ago. Lord knows, how you did it. Getting out to the ship and back, in time to go off duty? You've made me look a bloody idiot, Ned Machray!"

83

Then his shouting stopped. He walked into the workshop, sat on a seat of old tyres and put his head in his hands. "Do you know what makes it worse? The Chief Constable's daughter was listening. Floosie Rowena." He rubbed his eyes as if he was ready to weep. "I got a call from her at the end of the broadcast. She thinks you were 'fab', Ned. And she's going to tell her father."

PART TWO

THE ENTERTAINER

SEVEN

Hoboken Nights

The unveiling of Mollie Sweatman was celebrated after hours in the Hoboken Arms. Invited guests only. Ginger-bearded Gordon Freya had to be in the middle of it all because he had discovered the oil painting at the bottom of McKinley's shop but, at the last minute, he said he wouldn't turn up unless Shannelle promised to drink with him. "We're back together," the girl said to Timbers, again and again, and Timbers raised her eyes to Heaven.

Chloed, the Hoboken's landlady, wouldn't let me into the bar because I was in uniform but she said I could sit down to a midnight supper in the back kitchen. I laid my tunic on the flagstone floor and put my helmet on top. Then I pulled away my detachable shirt collar and addressed the fry up of left over food. I was open necked and had my sleeves rolled up but I wasn't comfy until I loosened my waistband and went up and down until the seat of my trousers sagged a little extra. I had a note from the Superintendent in my back pocket. 'You're under every stone I turn. See me!' It was neither typed nor handwritten in a careful script. Rickety capital letters had been dug into the scrap paper with a hard pencil. It looked venomous. It looked like a note written by a Superintendent on the edge. I kept it folded in my pocket in case I got chance to discuss it with someone friendly.

The fried feast was difficult to digest, so I stood up and walked around the table. I kept my back straight and kept puffing out. I could see through to the bar but I was looking from the kitchen, along the passage and into the smoky atmosphere of the saloon, so it was all blues and greys like a badly tuned television. Every so often someone walked through the door and closed it behind them. Then I had to wait for it to get opened again. It was hopeless. My picture of what was going on was hazy and interrupted. I was bothered because I could see Timbers sitting on a leather bench with Terry Morrison, Stuart's father. It was a corner bench where they could ignore the others. Timbers wasn't flirting as she normally did when she was looking for business. Morrison had stretched his arm along the back of the seat so that Timbers could fall into a cuddle if she wanted. She didn't. But she didn't say no, either.

I needed to hear what they were saying but the hubbub was like twenty voices channelled through twenty ear trumpets and dumped in a galvanised bucket behind my head. Wanting to get closer, I left the kitchen and walked along the passage but when I reached the cigarette machine someone shouted, "Great show, Mr Ned! We don't want all this beat music. It's Trad Dad, yeah!" Then Chloed came out and sent me back to the kitchen.

I saw that Timbers and Morrison were sitting by an open window, but I could hardly go outside and eavesdrop from the pavement. They were in a corner, however, and if I could lodge myself on the other side of the interior wall and perhaps open a window from there, I would be able to follow their conversation. That meant the end cubicle of the Ladies Toilet.

The Ladies in the Hoboken Arms are smaller than the Gents, although I have never noticed a good reason why. I decided not to sit down. Instead, I opened the frosted window and stood up against the corner pipe of the cubicle. I had brought my helmet with me in case anyone asked awkward questions.

Morrison wanted Timbers to keep young Stuart away from me, he said. He was sure that I would involve his son in a police intrigue that could only lead to trouble. Timbers said that the boy's father should stop stealing cigarettes from the dockyard.

The man's croaking irritated me; he had the cracked, hoarse tone of a man who has smoked himself dry. Timbers thought he was tough, rough and ready for it; I could tell that. But I knew Morrison was a reckless ne'er-do-well and she didn't need that sort of character in her life. God, it made me cringe to hear her make up to him. She was teasing, saying no and contradicting everything he said; that was Timbers' way of doing it but there was eagerness in her attitude. She couldn't let him go. For all his voiced concern about his young son, Morrison was all self, self, self. Hell, I wanted to twist his nose from his face.

I was trapped in the toilet – unable to interrupt them, unable to break them up. Every time I reached to open the cubicle door, a lady walked into the cloakroom.

I heard one enter the next cubicle. I heard her tinkle, then she did a bit more. Then she made a great fuss of struggling up with her knickers. Honestly, you would have thought that she was putting on a show. She left without pulling the chain. She spent a long time at the sink; she was probably fussing with her hair. She didn't wash her hands. I waited to hear her leave the cloakroom. Suddenly, she was rapping on my toilet door.

"Are you a man in there! Speak up!"

I stayed still.

"You, you, you little gerbil. You need flushing out. I shall fetch the janitor!"

I pictured her flouncing out so that the door closed with a bang. I secured my helmet on top and came out of the cubicle. A young woman walked in and gasped, covering her mouth with both hands.

"No, Miss. It's better to stay away. I'm investigating reports of an interloper."

I offered the same explanation when Chloed arrived, moments later. She didn't believe me. "Get back to the kitchen, Edward. You can help with some washing up before you leave."

As I emerged into the passage, Gordon Freya tagged onto me. Had I seen Shannelle, he asked. He hadn't seen her for half an hour.

I was shocked to see how much this man had deteriorated. Gordon Freya had never been a popular man. Girls, especially, didn't like him. But I remembered him as an old fashioned and well turned out character, often deep in thought. The man who followed me into the kitchen was sunken faced and round shouldered. He used to walk proudly; now he shuffled.

"You've not seen my Shannelle, have you?" he kept asking.

When I told him to sit down at the wooden table, he immediately recognised that I had been able to see Morrison and Timbers through the open doors. "Ah," he said. "You've noticed." Timbers had once described Gordon Freya's voice as a voice full of holes. Too many whispers, too many shallow breaths and too much thinking got in the way. "There are two types," he explained. "The watchers and the watched. The painters and those they paint. Sometimes, if the pieces match, they click together like pieces of a jigsaw puzzle. But sometimes, no. Sometimes the pieces jar." He demonstrated with fighting fingers. "And when a watcher and a watched join together, they never become one. Joined, but not one. Mr Machray, I am not a well man, you know that. There is bleeding inside of me."

I stopped him complaining. "Were you in the stew-house on the night of the murder?"

"You know that I wasn't. Outside, yes, looking after my Shannelle. But inside, no. Although sometimes it is hard to remember."

"How did Peacock find you?"

"He didn't find me. I told you, I was outside looking out for Shannelle. So, when I saw her in the police car, I collected her. What else would you have me do? I took her home; she should never have run away from me. She understands now." He massaged his temples. "I have headaches all the time," he explained.

I looked through to the bar. "You must be pleased with this evening."

"Why? Why should I be pleased? It's a horrible picture. And, I might say, a horrible woman, made more horrible if you should ever see her daughter without clothes."

"Her daughter?"

"Aunt Em. Didn't you know? Mollie Sweatman was Aunt Em's mother. Lord, have you seen her in there? She thinks she's chaperoning Maggie but everyone knows Maggie can look after herself. Em's dressed up to look like her mum. She's got a grey and silver turban and a plastic hairband on top that she's sprayed with child's glitter. She looks awful, Ned. She bought those sandals because they're like the ones in the picture and they don't fit her. She looks pitiful. Sad in a way that makes you feel sorry for old dears, all over."

But then his mind drifted from our conversation. He studied the tabletop as his fingernail scratched the old wood. "What does my

90

doctor know? I say, my head is bleeding inside but, because she can't see anything, she says I'm all right. She says, I'm not bleeding inside when every day I can feel it. Here, the blood is swelling the bridge of my nose." He put his fingertips between his eyes and squeezed. "I'll be dead before morning and my doctor won't take the blame. What does she know?"

His attention came back to me. "Can you remember what it was like, Machray, when the Hoboken was broken down and boarded up and everybody in Goodladies knew their business? A bookie's runner on every corner. Housewives bought stale goods and asked no questions. They were grateful for it because we still had rationing. It wasn't so long ago. You'd come back from the war and used to walk up and down when Sergeant Garrick was off. Do you remember when the tailor in Commercial Road was burgled in the night? The next term, the kids round here were the best turned out for school. Like posh grammar school kids, they were. I used to come down here at night, from my home on the outskirts of the city – my clean, well furnished home – and I'd love the realness of Goodladies and her people. I'd sketch them. I'd stand on the street corners and I'd sketch them. The housewives, the bookies' runners and the tarts. Especially the tarts. They were different in those days. Machray, let's see if we can remember them."

"Aunt Em," I said. "She did as much business as any of them."

"Yes. She was forty already, wasn't she? And Irish Dowell's mother."

"Do you remember Heinie?" I asked. "Heinie, the Mill Worker."

"Good Lord," he said. "I'd forgotten her. So many of the names have gone, Ned, but I still have friends, you know. People think that I'm on my own with no-one to talk to but that's not true. I sit with Berkeley most afternoons. You know Berkeley? He has very strong ideas and he's very well read. He knows all about the Common Market. He's never been married. For forty years he's hated women so you'd expect him to be well read. And your Piggy Tucker – she's always seeking me out, wanting to know what I think about current talk. Is it true 'Gau-dunne', she'll say. She says my name just like my poor wife used to. Have you noticed that, Ned? She says 'Gau-dunne, the talk is Ned's got eyes for a new policewoman. Is it true?'"

"Don't call her 'My Piggy Tucker'. She's not mine."

"Please, I didn't mean to put you out." He unfolded his tobacco pouch and produced a blank card. "Shall I tell you the difference between the old days and now?"

I shook my head. He played with the card as he spoke, turning it over and over. "Piano players. In the old days, piano players were at the centre of things. Now, the girls like to show off, with their fashions and flirting. Look at them, strutting around, all over the bar, and the piano player sits in the corner. No-one takes any notice. Mind, the music's not the same, Ned. You'd know about that, being a music man. The songs aren't there."

"Gordon," I began cautiously. "The Walking Stick Man was looking for Shannelle, that night, because he knew you."

"Not for ten years, he didn't," Freya replied. "He was down here in the fifties and he used to sit with Berkeley and me. I showed him some of my drawings and he liked them. No, he did, really. He even made them up into a little book for me. All leather bound; it was lovely. I must let you see it." He looked at the card, repeatedly checking that it was blank. "You must have killed him," he said. "As good as."

The accusation made no sense. "Why do you think I killed him, Gordon?"

"As good as, I said. Who could have told him about the Curiosity Shop? And who told him that Shannelle and I had been living together? There was only you and I to tell him, Ned. He didn't know anyone else to ask. He didn't talk to me, so he must have spoken to you. Is that it, Ned? Did you tell him to look for Shannelle in the Curiosity Shop?"

"I didn't know him. I've never spoken to him."

"He would have remembered you, Ned. From the old days. An old copper. I think you as good as killed him." Freya was saying these things in a quiet, mild voice. He was still fiddling with the card. "I won't tell anyone," he said.

I argued that the Walking Stick Man could have asked questions in any of the pubs along Goodladies Road. Old landladies, like Rusty and Irish Dowell, could have told him all that he wanted to know.

But Freya shook his head. "He wouldn't have done it like that. He wouldn't have done it in public until he was sure of his ground.

That's the way he was." Then, with a little embarrassment, he pushed the card towards me. "Can I have your autograph? I've got a pen somewhere, I know I have." He was patting his pockets. The hesitation got the better of him and he snatched the card and ripped it up. "This is silly! I know you too well! I'm sorry. Ned, I'm sorry."

I picked up my tunic from the floor and took out my official pocket book. I ripped out one of the pages. (Each page was numbered so that even a cursory check would determine if any evidence had been tampered with.) I wrote in large letters 'To Gordon with Best Wishes from Ned D.J. Machray.'[2]

The gesture brought tears to his eyes. "Oh, thank you, Ned," he kept saying. He got to his feet, still fussing. "I'm going to find Shannelle. I can't allow her to stand on the street corners anymore. She must learn that she's mine, for keeps." He left by the back door.

I went to the big sink and watched through the window as he walked through the wooden side gate and into the streets.

* * *

Dorothy Rose 'Ruby' Redinutt leant against the radiator in the empty bedroom and didn't know what to do. She wanted to undress and climb onto the bed so that she could be ready and waiting when the man walked through the door. But Timberdick had taken the blankets away. 'They'll get in the way, Pet, and men fall asleep if they get too warm. That's the last thing you want. Sicking up on you's worse, but nothing else.' And, blankets or no blankets, Ruby thought that she ought not to undress until he was there to watch. Even if she couldn't do a striptease (and, boy, how she couldn't!) he'd still want to see her take off her clothes. It was part of what he was paying for, Ruby thought.

---

[2]In the 1990's, my carer pushed me through an antiques fair where I found this autograph slip mounted with an old photograph of myself. The little lady at the bookstall said that Ned 'D.J.' Machray was a cult radio celebrity from the 1960's and well worth £20. I didn't tell her the truth but I didn't part with my money, either. I have often wondered how that page from my pocket book travelled through the thirty years. I know that it was in Freya's trousers when he left the Hoboken Arms.

93

"So," she sighed aloud and clapped her hands to her sides. Aimlessly. She walked to the dressing table and poked at her hair. Twenty minutes early and nothing to do but worry about it. Silly really.

"Well, then."

At least, she could wash herself and make sure that she was absolutely clean and sweetly smelling when he touched her. But, she had done all that.

"Done all that," she confirmed as she backed away from the mirror. A room with its own bathroom – pom, pom, pom – must be the most expensive in the house. Pom, pom, pom. Well, it's there to be used. Timberdick would expect her to use it.

But what if he knocked on the door when she was undressed in the bathroom? Well, she'd call out for him to wait. But then he would think that she was on the toilet and his first picture of her would be coarse.

He knocked.

Immediately, her arms went across her stomach supporting the weight of her bosom. "Who is it?" She was standing in the middle of the carpet.

He knocked again.

Surely, he wouldn't be this early?

When he knocked for a third time without announcing himself, Ruby stepped forward and opened the door.

"You!" she said. Accusing rather than welcoming. "You're the boy who held Timberdick upside down!"

David Barton kept his thoughts to himself. He wasn't a 'boy'. He didn't live at home any more. He had moved into lodgings above the butcher's shop where he worked. All right, his mother still kept an eye on him. Cooked his supper every night and checked that his bed was aired. But he wasn't a 'boy'. Perhaps he was odd. Yes, he'd agree. He did things that thirty year olds didn't do. He spent hours in the library copying extracts into exercise books. And he had the best index of names on park benches in the city. So, he was 'peculiar', maybe. And his trouble with girls wouldn't be a trouble at all, if only they would listen.

Ruby thought he was funny shaped. His shoulders were too

broad for his head, hips and ankles, yet his chest was so powerful – beefed up, she called it – that everything else seemed out of proportion. His fine hair, his pale watery eyes and flaky complexion and the bum fluff on his face made him look underdone. Ruby – now being her dirty new self – wondered what else would be small and sparsely nested. But he's clean, she thought. Small and delicately drawn and clean. Well washed hands, close cut nails, and properly soaped behind the ears.

Ruby was relieved. She knew that she could cope with this one and, from now on, the evening would be easy. In less than an hour, Dorothy Rose – the unfortunate cousin in every family – would be gone for good. Completely.

"I'm glad it's you," she said, remembering Timbers' instructions to welcome him.

"What did you tell the detectives?" he asked without introduction.

Ruby was too disappointed to reply. Here she was, in a pub's bedroom and ready to take her clothes off for money. Wasn't that sufficient a statement that she did not want men to see her as a policewoman? Lord, it had taken all her gumption to get this far, only to hear her first customer ask about police work.

"I haven't told them anything. Nobody's asked me any questions."

"What –"

" – And if they did, I've nothing to tell them."

"What do you know about that evening? About me?" He pushed forward so that Ruby was soon up against the radiator and the window.

"Nothing."

"I couldn't bear it if people knew I was in stockings. Did you know about that?"

"Not until you just told me. And it really doesn't matter, if you enjoyed it."

"I did." He turned away, allowing her to come forward into the room again. "But I get angry every time I think about people talking behind my back. My mother was there for an hour before the dead man came. Do you think she knows it was me in the loft?" He demanded, "I want you to question me. I was upstairs when the Walking Stick Man was killed. I could have killed him. I want you to question me."

"I can't do that," she said gently. "I wouldn't know what to ask and, besides, I'm not being a policewoman at the moment, am I?"

It wasn't supposed to be like this. Two days ago, she had asked Timberdick, 'What's it like to be taken by a man you don't know?' Although the wise prostitute hadn't given an encouraging answer, Ruby still expected the thrill of submitting to a stranger. But now David and Ruby had talked to each other, they had formed opinions. They had each decided, to their own degrees, if they liked the other. This wasn't what Ruby was looking for.

"I know you were there," he said. "I saw you on the street corner at nine and you were still there when I looked out of the upstairs windows. And, you were first on the scene – just minutes after it happened. I don't think you went away at all. I think you were standing outside the stew-house all night."

But Ruby did not want to talk about the murder. She nearly asked, 'What would you like to do with me?' She had made up her mind to be as obliging as he wanted. After all, it was her maiden voyage and she had so much to learn. She said, "I'm ready."

He didn't respond at once, but turned his back and, after a few moments, sat down at the dressing table mirror. "You're not going to talk to me, are you? You can't know what it's like, having it with girls who won't talk to you properly. Really, really pretty girls. With bodies out of magazines and films and advertisements — but they won't talk." He thumped his knees to make his point. "I want to explain simple things to them, but they have to be cold. Always. They don't understand how cold they are. They're loving, I suppose, in the way they've learned. They whisper and praise you and Layna and Shannelle always take their time. They're patient with me. But, no warmth. I could be someone else, for all they care. Care? I don't want them to care but I want them to help me. Help me say what I want."

"What do you want them to do?"

"Different things with different girls. Different places. Different times, even. I mean, it's bound to be different, isn't it?"

96

"What would you like to do with me?"

He wrung his hands. Right, say it David. Staring into the mirror, he began, "Take everything off except your dress – and pull it down to your waist so that it's like a skirt. Then kneel on all fours on the bed."

"So that my pear drops are hanging down, waiting to be picked?" She moved to loosen the zip at her back.

"Don't do it now! Don't be like all the others. Don't spoil it from the start. Wait until I've told you everything." But he couldn't remember all the details that he wanted to say and he was getting cross with himself. He squeezed his knuckles as he said, "I want you to do it while I'm not looking. Then tell me when you've done it."

Ruby suggested, "You tell me what to do. Then give me the money. Then, I'll get ready while you look the other way. And I'll say when you can turn around."

He nodded. "Yes. I'll hear you take off your clothes and climb onto the mattress. You see, that's what it is for me. Hearing you, with pictures in my head."

In this way, and knowing that he would peek in the mirror, Dorothy Rose embarked upon her new life. She went slowly through his procedure, not talking but making more noise than she needed to. Only a few minutes later, she was kneeling on all fours on the bed, her head at the foot and the top of her dress pulled down. Suddenly, he spun round from the dressing table. He knees went to the carpet with a thud. Now they were face to face and close enough to kiss.

He accused her. "You were outside the murder house all night. Why? Waiting for someone, I think. Wanting something to happen."

"I – I wanted to join in with the girls, but I was too scared to ask," she replied nervously. She could explain things easily, she wanted to say, but not while she was looking so ridiculous. On the bed and half exposed. The situation made her sound uncertain. Guilty. "Things are different now," she said lamely.

"No. I think you're telling lies, W.P.C. Redinutt. I think you were there as a great big secret."

Ruby didn't answer. She closed her eyes and, in her head, pleaded, 'Please. Please, get on with it.' The whole thing had been spoilt. It was nothing like her daydreams.

But when Timbers and Shannelle walked into the bedroom, twenty minutes later, Ruby couldn't keep the desperate edge out of her voice. "What did he say? Did he say it was good, I mean, I was good?" It still mattered to her.

David had left and Ruby was busy in the bathroom. The girlfriends smiled at each other and arranged themselves side by side on the big bed. "Ah, the men I have known on this," Timbers sighed.

"Like Silverfish?" asked Shannelle. She spoke up so that the girl could hear in the bathroom. "Your Superintendent before this one, Ruby, was called Silverfish. He was one of Timbers' regulars."

Timberdick said, "He used to like me on the carpet in front of that radiator. He kept a razor hidden in the bathroom and I used to shave men's backsides with it between his visits. He never knew."

"Stop it, you two!" Ruby called through. "Stop teasing me! And tell me what David said." Ruby came out of the bathroom. "Come on, you little cows. Tell me." She was wearing a pleated skirt, stockings and shoes and a very clean bra encasing her very large breasts.

"Jeepers," said Shannelle, looking fixedly at them. "They're better out of uniform."

Ruby folded her arms and stood, feet apart, at the bottom of the heavy old bedstead. "I must have been good, or he would have said and you would have said."

The lovebirds on the bed said nothing. (Ruby wasn't sure about them, but they were glancing and smiling at each other like lovebirds at rest.) "Well, if you haven't got anything to say to me," she said. "Well, I certainly have got a message for you. David said I should tell you."

"What?" said the two together.

"That his mother was at the Curiosity Shop and hour before the dead man."

"The dead man?" queried Shannelle.

"The man who died."

"And what? Aunt Emmie was there?" asked Timbers, sitting up.

"What difference does that make?" Shannelle snapped. "Don't listen to her, Timbers."

"I'm not saying it's important," said Ruby. "David told me to tell you, that's all."

"So you're not the police anymore," said Timbers. "Or he'd have meant the message for you, not us."

"Yes," said Ruby, very pleased. "I mean, no. I suppose I'm not."

Shannelle sat up. (Her legs were too stumpy to reach the floor from the side of the mattress.) She was cross. "God, I've had enough of this murder. I was there and I saw the man die. I wish people would remember that."

"She would have been with Gordon Freya, then." Timbers said evenly. "If she was there an hour before. Was she coming or going?"

"David didn't say."

"Going, of course," said Shannelle, still unhappy. "Coming makes no sense, Timbers."

"You're right, but I'd better make sure. I better ask your Gordon." Timbers stood up and walked from the bed to the door. She said to Ruby, "David wants to see you next week. You must have been very good because he can only afford Layna once a month. If that, sometimes."

Then, before she left the room, Shannelle rushed to her and grabbed her bony arm. "Leave Gordon alone, Timbers. He's changed. I promise you, he's different now."

Freya had been out in the night for half an hour before Timberdick left the Hoboken. She didn't see me standing on the corner of Cardrew Street, about fifty yards away. I watched her hesitate in the middle of the road. Then she hurried to check the row of garages behind the pub but emerged after only a few minutes. He wasn't there. Cleverly, she worked out that while Shannelle remained in the Hoboken her lover would eventually return for her. So, Timberdick waited on the little bit of pavement that had been her pitch for so many years.

I reflected that I hadn't seen her standing there for months but now she made a picture that brought together all the seasons through which I had known her. The skinny woman in white high-heeled shoes. The dirty white raincoat that was deliberately too short. Stockings, always the colour of rich tea. She seemed so much a part of that street corner that her presence provided an odd comfort. If Timberdick was at her station, then little could be wrong with the world.

An old Morris Oxford drew up, almost immediately. She stepped forward and explained that she was already waiting for someone. When she withdrew to the dark edge of the pavement, the driver called her back and, without much thought, Timberdick agreed to his second suggestion. She got in the car and the driver steered them into the side street. Out of my sight.

I checked my watch. I had been off duty for almost two hours and shouldn't have been standing on the street in uniform. I made up my mind to wander home but, after less than two minutes, Timbers walked back to her corner. Her clothes hadn't been disturbed. She carried loose change in her hand and kept swapping it from one to the other. I decided to speak with her.

Then I saw Morrison leave the Hoboken and Timberdick was, straightaway, fidgeting on her feet. I felt my collar tighten with jealousy. Timberdick had never fidgeted for me. Morrison crossed the empty road junction.

"It'd cost you," she said quietly.

The man stopped, not yet on the kerb, his hands still in his trouser pockets. "Who says I'd want to?"

"Nobody. I was just saying, it'd cost you. OK, I know your lad and we've been talking about him, so I was just saying that it'd make no difference. You'd still have to pay me."

He shook his head and laughed, dismissing her confidence as impertinence. He walked on but stopped again and turned before he was properly down the side street.

"Twelve quid," she said before he asked. "A tenner if you're happy to do it in the street." She had no intention of letting him do anything, but she wanted to make it clear that he wasn't special. Their conversation in the pub had prompted no favour.

"Yeah, all right," he said. "'Cept I know a house in Cardrew Street. Come on. Don't worry, you'll get your twelve quid."

He grabbed her bony white hand and hurried her along the old brick path that connected the two back streets. They didn't see the black-coated man run across the junction. He laughed at them. He was neither threatening nor intrusive, but there was something naughty about him. Something gleeful in his furtiveness. A fanciful mind might have called him an imp or goblin. I hurried to the middle of the junction- where three streets come together and the lights of the Hoboken spill across the crumbling tarmac – but he was already running off towards the old Methodist rooms.

"Hey!" I shouted.

The night-time character kept running, acknowledging my challenge with only a squawkish cackle. Bugger McKinley's ghost was a game, I decided.

In Cardrew Street, Terry Morrison found a back door key wedged between old bricks and a gutter. "Now, keep quiet. Tommy and Smee are out, and we're allowed in, but there's no knowing who else is here."

She followed him inside. "I'm not going upstairs," Timbers said as they crept through the dark unfamiliar kitchen. Timbers was aware of the woman's cooking tools on the table and her tea towels hanging from the draining board, and that Timbers shouldn't be here. "Look this is sick. Doing it on someone else's bed when they don't know. It's like using their toilet and not pulling the chain."

He grinned. "Since when did Timbers pull the chain?"

They got as far as the stairs. Still, they hadn't switched on any lights. Timbers noticed slippers next to a door, change on a table and a coat draped over the banister post. This house was another family's home and the folk who loved it had no warning of Timberdick's visit. "I don't care, Terry Morrison," she whispered (because Heaven forbid that someone should hear them). "You can be as clever as you like, but I'm not going up to the bedroom."

"Fine. We'll do it here."

"Look, no. Look—" She had never reneged on a client before. She knew she had been stupid and talked her way into a corner. "Look, I'm pregnant, Terry, and I don't want to do it."

Immediately, he took his hands from her shoulders. "Bloody hell! You're having a baby?" He stepped back. After all, the disease might be catching. "Who's – no, I guess you wouldn't know."

Timbers sat on the stairs. "I do need to find a father, Tel. God, don't look so scared. I'd never choose you. And I need to get off the streets."

"You can't stop working," he said. "It's all you can do."

"I know that. Your boy's made it clear to me. But I need to get off the streets. My baby will start school in 1971. I don't want her

101

mother to be standing on Goodladies Road when she does. 1971, Tel. That's my date."

He said it sounded like an age away.

Then Timbers caught sight of a shape in the frosted window of the front door. "There!" she shouted. "A man in a black coat."

The letterbox flapped, letting in an inane laugh. "Yes, I'm the man in the black coat!" the mystery figure taunted.

Morrison turned around, confused.

"A man in black, trying to look at us through the front door!" Timbers explained. "Stay here, Terry. I'm off to chase Bugger McKinley's ghost."

* * *

I saw Timberdick leave Smee Ditchen's place at midnight. I decided to wait for her new boyfriend. I didn't want to fight with him but he needed putting straight. So, I kept in the shadows and waited for her to pass. She was in too much of a hurry to notice me.

I thought I was well hidden, but an old married couple called from the other side of the road. "Play some Bilk, Mr Ned! The best of Ball, Barber and Bilk. Play it for us on your next show. Say it's for Mr and Mrs Benn."

I thanked them.

"Great show!"

I thanked them again.

As they started to cross the road to shake my hand, a sash window clattered open, up the street. A man in his pyjamas leaned out and shouted, "It's Dee Jay Machray!" And, somewhere, a cornet released one long, shivering, note.

Before I realised what was happening, half a dozen neighbours had come out of their houses.

"Do you know Mike A?" asked a young wife with a housecoat wrapped around a pyjamas top. She had mules on, but nothing else.

"Mike A?"

"Mike Aherne. He's on Caroline in the mornings and we'd love him to come to our beetle drive on Thursday."

I said I didn't know him and she said it started at three o'clock.

"Hey, Mack! How do you get out there?" called the man at the far window. "Some sort of launch, is it? Takes you three miles out to the ship, is that it?"

Now more bedroom lights went on. Another window opened and a teenager shouted, "They call it a tender, Mr Evans."

"Who's let this bloody bird out!" An old woman's protest brought a cheer from the rest of the street. "Who else has to sleep with a bloody budgerigar flying around the bedroom? You get back in here, Barmy Evans."

Quietly, an army Corporal pushed an envelope into my hand. "Can you sign this, Mr Machray? It's for my daughter in America and she's heard all about Radio Caroline."

"He's not on Caroline," explained the girl in the housecoat.

"I know," said the Corporal. "But it's just as famous. Pirate radio ships, Mr Machray. They're all part of history now, you know. There'll be no stopping them. I've got you on tape, Mr Machray."[3]

Then the cornet player came into his own. A lean and hairless young man, wearing nothing but his pyjamas bottoms, stood at his front door and announced, "Opus for Mr Ned!" I recognised the first few notes of Stranger On The Shore but then his awful improvisation spiralled into a stew of lost notes and ragged rhythms.

He woke the street. It was well past midnight but a toddler came out on this scooter and an old couple, in overcoats, scarves and fur-lined booties, left home to walk their dog. By now, the crowd of my fans was too large for the pavement. Half undressed people pushed forward for my autograph. Others seemed to be tugging at my shirt and trousers as if they wanted to take a piece of me home. The boys shouted questions about jazz –sometimes no questions but the names of songs and players for which they wanted to express some sort of loyalty. I didn't understand what was going on, but clearly it was too

[3]When Timberdick died in 1970, her boyfriend found a tape of Sean's radio programme. It was in a shoebox with rude photographs of Shannelle and Baz Shipley. The tape later emerged as a bootleg cassette but it's not a genuine aircheck. Sean put it together in a local studio a month after his last broadcast. It was rough and ready. A bit of fun. I don't think that any recordings of his pirate radio station have survived. I have looked for his original tape of my jazz selection. I think it burned with the Hoboken Arms in 1966.

103

late for Ned Machray to declare that he wasn't a proper disc jockey; he had been tricked into it. And all the time, I felt an uneasiness that the incident was getting out of hand. There could not have been more than thirty in the crowd but too many people were too excited and they didn't know what they wanted. The cries of 'Mr Ned, Mr Ned,' became shrill and urgent. The smaller ones were being pushed and pulled. I saw a man stumble over the kerbstone, grazing his knee through a hole in his pyjamas. As I tried to get to him, a woman in a tight pink jumper and a miniskirt threw her arms around my neck and kissed me on the lips. People tried to pull her off but she wouldn't let go. Then another pair of arms wrapped itself around my neck. I remember thinking, 'I'm going to get hurt. I'm not Tommy Steele, for God's Sake.'

In the middle of this commotion, a posh new car drove down the road at speed. Everyone complained. 'Bloody liberty!' 'What's up with him?' 'Coming like that in our street. Doesn't he know it's dark?' The driver braked heavily, twenty yards from me and askew in the carriageway. Then he reversed with a great noise from the engine.

I hoped that he hadn't seen me because I didn't like being a policeman for posh people. They always addressed me by my surname. 'Look here, Machray.' As if I was some sort of groom or house porter.

But it was worse than that.

It was my Superintendent.

He'd been dining out and was clearly the worse for wear. He climbed out of the car – his sleeves screwed up, his dress shirt open at the front. "Now, look here!" he started, jabbing a finger at my face. "I want you to know, I'm in on your story."

I saw the army Corporal coming forward to punch him. I fitted my hands against the ribs in the pink jumper and pushed her into the soldier's arms. She laughed. In some odd way, being tossed from one to the other had thrilled her. It seemed to break the spell of the gathering hysteria. Some people thought that I had grabbed her breasts, but I hadn't. I had only felt her ribs. Embarrassed, they turned away from me and challenged the Superintendent. He took no notice of them at first – it was as if he hadn't seen them – but when they went 'Ooh' and 'Bad news' and 'Surely not', he put the pointing finger away. He reduced his words to a whisper and, putting an arm around my shoulders, led me away, just a few feet.

The Corporal hunched his shoulders and walked away. Others followed him, but I remained aware of Barmy Evans still looking from his bedroom window.

"I understand, P.C. Machray," said the Superintendent. "I was dining tonight with someone from your London office. He talked rather too much, I'm afraid, and let me in on your secrets before I could stop him."

I put two fingers in to stretch my shirt collar. I had learned to be nervous of ideas from London. "Sir, I don't know what you are talking about."

"They want to requisition an aircraft carrier."

Oh, bugger.

"They want to park it off the East African coast."

Oh, Lord.

"And broadcast propaganda to Rhodesia."

Oh God, please don't let this happen to me. They will leave me there. They'll anchor me in the Indian Ocean and, twenty years later, someone will find a rusting hulk with my bones braced around the ship-to-shore radio. "Isn't that a job for the BBC. The World Service and all that."

"Wise men don't think so. The BBC must be allowed clean hands in this business. The Corporation is independent. Only the Government does propaganda. They've established a smoke screen by taking advice from these new pirate radio stations. Radio London, Radio Caroline and the others. But the most promising operator is a one and nine penny affair that broadcasts haphazardly off our coast, Ned. To you and I, this is a ramshackle affair that sends out programmes for two hours here and there. No real schedule. And no real power to their transmitter. But the wise men say they have the best suited style for what we need."

He slapped me round the shoulders. "I'll be honest with you, Constable. When I heard that you had been out there, on the seas, playing jazz records, wanting to be Keith Fordyce, I said, this man has gone too far. But now I see that it was all for Queen and Country. Machray, I'm damn proud of you. Damn, damn proud."

EIGHT

Piggy Tucker's Crime

Goodladies was a quarter of dark twists and turns where a door, built to face a road a hundred years ago, now faced nothing at all but was skew-whiff to a back path. A dray yard stayed on after the brewery had gone, its old cellar providing steps down to a jitty between two places where nobody wanted to go. The alleys and footpaths had corners for reasons lost in time; little alcoves that provided hiding places and rubbish dumps. At every turn you could find bricks and slates left over from jobs, hosepipes and wheels stowed away – safely at first because everyone knew where the owners were. Now the owners or their ideas had passed on, forgotten. Some houses had windows that were half below the pavement. Roads were sometimes too low so that four or five doors in a row needed extra steps, and the steps got in the way of the pavements. 'Hangman's Noose' was a loading arm that used to haul sacks to a first floor warehouse. Now, the warehouse was an upstairs cycle shed for workers using the railway across the street.

Bugger McKinley's ghost knew every nip and tuck. On nights when he was out, he would hide so that a passing headlight or a walker's torch would catch his face for a moment. He'd be there – seen but then not seen – and gone.

He scurried along pavements and across roads, a little man with legs that seemed to rotate like pedals rather than stride. He skipped from one set of shadows to the next so that Timbers chased him, then lost him, then caught sight of him again but never seemed to make up the ground between them. The silly giggle was never far away. Sometimes it seemed to rattle through the air as if it had come from nowhere. This ghost was good at it. Once, she thought she had outsmarted him. She guessed that he was heading for the railway lines so she ignored the glimpses and giggles that were meant to pull her this way and that, and she hurried directly to the concrete steps at the end of Rossington Street.

She caught sight of him in the twitchel by the railway lines but that lane can be quite a climb and, by the time she reached the footbridge, she thought he had given her the slip. Then he called out to her from the trees on the far bank and she chased him. Across the Secondary Modern's playground. Up to Goodladies Junction and back down to the Methodist Rooms. There, Terry Morrison, joined in.

"I'll get him," shouted Terry.

"Just talk to him," Timbers pleaded.

He was heading for the greyhound stadium but twice they lost him and only got the scent again when he stood still and called for them. But the game went on too long and even the wiry ghost grew tired. Timbers saw him wobble as he crossed the road to Jack's Café and Old Moore's Lane.

"I'm not the ghost," Gordon Freya panted when Timbers was only yards behind.

As he turned into the cobbled lane, a figure leapt from the darkness. A girl, no older than fifteen, in black stockings stretched to their limit across her fat thighs, and wearing a grubby miniskirt creased and rubbed by her every step and bend. Her brown hair was lanky and flat. "Bloody hell, man!" She stood her ground. Freya turned on his ankle and went down to the ground, smacking his head against the café's brick wall.

Timberdick and Terry were with him immediately. Timbers knelt beside the casualty and pulled his shirt-tail from his trouser waist so that she could dab at the blood on his face.

"Urh!" screamed the fat girl. "Urh! Awful!"

He had gashed his forehead in the wrong spot for bright red blood poured down his face, making a tacky padding in his whiskers and giving the accident more drama than it deserved.

"I'm not the ghost," he repeated. "He fooled you at the railway bridge. That's where you lost him."

The girl waddled off, turning around to call Timberdick a 'scabby cow' before she disappeared around the corner.

"What were you doing, Mr Freya, running away like that? Terry, go into the café and get something for his head. A cushion or a blanket or towels."

Freya couldn't open his eyes; there was too much blood. "I wanted you to follow me."

"You led us away from the ghost, is that it?"

"No. I wanted you to follow me into the dark so that I could make you talk. You've stolen my book, Timberdick. I know you've got it."

"What book?"

"The drawings I did. Drawings of girls when I first came to Goodladies. You remember it, or you've heard about it, or – God Timbers, no-one else could have taken it except you."

"I don't know what you're talking about. What's this book?"

"I hid it in the church. No-one could have found it unless they spent hours and hours looking for it."

Timbers smiled. "Mr Freya, I haven't got your book but I can guess who has."

Terry returned, his arms full of cloths and towels. Jack, the café owner, stomped behind him, telling everyone to get the injured man out of the way. They couldn't let him stay here, he pleaded. The All Night Café couldn't put up with thugs and whores.

Timbers ignored the fuss. "Who's got Bugger's raincoat, Freya? What's it all about? Who's the ghost?"

He closed his eyes. "Wander the streets, Timbers," he said mildly. "Let the ghost tease you."

Piggy Tucker had watched it all from the café. She waited until people had left him alone on the cobbles. Then she took him to her room in the greyhound stadium. Between the Ladies and Gents that she cleaned four nights a week. It was supposed to be her storeroom but she had so mothered it that it resembled, if not her sittingroom, at least a comfy hidey-hole. She left him in the old armchair with a broken back while she went next door for toilet tissue and paper towels. She patched him up as best she could. He felt like the casualty in the nursery rhyme, made better with vinegar and brown paper.

"I told you!" Gordon Freya thumped his knees and chanted. "I told you. I told you. I told you." Piggy Tucker wiped his face with a cold flannel. "They want to chase me off the earth," he said. "Like an evil vampire who needs to be laid bare and stuck, so that he cannot rise up again."

"Gau-dunne," she pleaded. She knew that she could help him by adopting the intonation that his wife used to employ. She whispered it and ran her fingers through his damp hair. "You're not a vampire," she told him.

"My eyes are bleeding again," he countered. "I can feel the backs of them bleeding into my head. It's happened before, you know that."

"No. No, I know nothing of the sort. I've told you lots of times; it's all Timbers' fault. She makes us cry and she wants us to blame ourselves, doesn't she? Oh, she's made me cry, Gau-dunne. Haven't I told you stories of how she's made me cry?"

"She says I'm Bugger McKinley's ghost."

"There. What do you see? She's making you think bad things about yourself. And she calls your Piggy 'Toilet Brush' so that other people will think that I'm rubbish. Gau-dunne, you must help me put things right. We know that she killed the Walking Stick Man, don't we? I've explained that to you many times, haven't I?"

Over and over, she had.

"And you must tell me things that poor Shannelle has said. What did Timbers do that night? What happened to Shannelle?"

"She's a naughty girl too," he whispered as he tried to puzzle things out in his head.

"But we'll forgive Shannelle, won't we? We've said that. How many times?"

Gordon nodded. Yes, over and over.

"But Timbers, Gau-dunne. You must tell me how we can get Timberdick in trouble."

* * *

The telephone was ringing and – at two in the morning – the household knew that the call would be for the Chief Inspector. Bernie Trent was already putting on his slippers and wrapping a dressing gown over his pyjamas, but he was too polite to venture from the little bedroom. Mrs Tegg should answer the phone, not her lodger. Mrs Tegg, because Mister did not want another man to see him in his nightclothes.

Doreen knocked and said, "It's a lady, Bernard, with information." Trent replied without opening the bedroom door and, after he had heard the Tegg's room door close, he went to the telephone at the bottom of the stairs.

However, all this care in avoiding another man in the night came to nought, because the detective had to knock on Rennie and Doreen's bedroom door before the house could settle again.

"Come in."

When Trent poked his head inside, he found a bedroom dimly lit by a streetlamp through open curtains. Rennie was sitting at the foot of the mattress, smoking in his pyjamas bottoms, and Doreen was sitting up in bed. Her arm crossed properly over her chest. Her hair was in curlers. Her face was dusty white.

"Where would I find Old Moore's Gate?" he asked.

"It's a hole in the fence at the bottom of Moore's Lane," said Rennie between puffs. "People get into the dog-track that way. Go to the bottom of Goodladies Road and–"

"Yes, I know the way to the stadium."

"You know Jack's All Night Café? Well, Moore's Lane runs down the side."

"Thank you." And he thanked Doreen as well, excusing his intrusion. "I'll not be back before morning so I'll not disturb you again. Thank you."

It was a cold night. As Trent crossed the web of Victorian streets, he captured the geography of the place but none of its romance. The images of a dirty city sparked no curiosity and, especially, no wish to reach out and touch it. A drunk in an open camel hair coat lay behind the steering wheel of an old American car; the door open, one foot at the end of an ankle probing for the ground. In another street, a teenage girl was pressed up against a well-dressed man, three times her age. His broad shoulders leaned against a family's front door. A couple of yards to their left, a second man waited, smoking heavily, keeping the smoke out of his eyes as he checked his watch. Dogs copulated at the end of the street. Trent didn't think that these pictures were bad, but he wanted nothing to do with the place.

When the Chief Inspector walked into Jack's All Night Café, the place was without a customer. Marching music was playing from a tape recorder and Jack was asleep behind the counter. Irritable that any night worker should nap on duty – policeman or not – the Chief rapped on the counter and shouted, "Tea!"

The word, like a bursting balloon, woke the proprietor with a jolt. "Good Lord, sir, I'm sorry."

Trent leant on the counter, deliberately making himself as large as possible in Jack's face. "I'll have five cigarettes and a match," he demanded.

"I don't sell 'em loose, sir."

"People say you do. Navy duty frees. You take them out the packets and sell them in twists of paper – five at a time – with a match pushed in."

"I don't know what you mean. Sir, you're Mr Trent, aren't you? Ned's new boss."

"You do know what I mean."

Jack went beneath the counter and produced two hundred cigarettes in packs of twenty. "It's not fair. You taxing me like this. Mr Trent, I want to keep you happy. I want to keep all policemen happy. I want to keep everyone happy. Bookies, taxi-men, porters – anyone except tarts like whippets. Bloody giggling on, like they do. You ask old Ned, I'm not out for any trouble."

The Chief Inspector looked at the cigarettes on the counter. He didn't touch them. "You can tell your supplier that I'm going to close him down. Either, I'll put him in gaol or I'll scare the pants off his outlets. Either way, you tell him that the Chief's after him. Yes, Ned Machray's new boss is going to get him."

"I – I don't – Mr Trent, this is Revenue business. What's it got to do with the police?"

"Stolen goods, Jack."

"Good God, Mr Trent, I didn't know. I mean, you ask Ned. He'll tell you that I'll have nothing to do with stolen goods." He snatched the two hundred back. "I'm not even letting you have them."

"Tea," Trent said sharply and withdrew to a table by the window.

111

Presently, without a word, Jack put the mug of tea on the counter but didn't deliver it, at first. He told people that he never did. He wasn't here to wait on tables, he said. He sunk back in his armchair and kept out of sight. Then, after a few minutes and still not saying anything, he brought the drink to the Chief Inspector's table.

It was twenty minutes before he saw the dumpy, well-coated figure at the café window. She tapped, and crooked a finger at him. Trent finished his tea, taking his time. Then he stood up, opening and closing his coat to make sure he was properly wrapped up before he walked out into the cold.

She took him down the lane. "We've not met, Chief Inspector, but I'm the lady that lives with P.C. Machray."

"You said as much on the phone, Miss Tucker. What do you want to tell me?"

"Timberdick Woodcock. The old woman who runs the brothel where the man was murdered."

"Old woman? That would be Mrs McKinley, the widow."

"No, I mean Timberdick. The skinny whore with a face like a sick rabbit or a crow, or a bald chicken. She's got no chin and her teeth stick out and her eyes are too big for their sockets."

"I think Miss Woodcock is thirty-five. Hardly 'old' I'd say."

Piggy tried to keep her patience. "Well, let's not argue about it. People are always making excuses for her. Always 'liking her a bit.' A bit more than they should, I say." She would have carried on but a goods train rattled across the viaduct behind them and Piggy and the Chief Inspector had to stand looking at each other without talking.

Then, "What do you want to tell me?" the Chief repeated wearily.

"Timberdick took a front door key from the body. Now, she wouldn't have done that if she hadn't known the door it would fit. So, she knew where the man lived, so she probably had a reason to kill him. So, probably did. Kill him, I mean."

Trent put his hands in his coat pockets. "It's very cold to be standing here, Miss Tucker. Cold and it's late."

"Of course, you're going to make excuses for her and say –"

"I'll say – how do you know about the key?"

"Because Shannelle was there. She saw Timbers pinch the key. And she told Gordon Freya because she lives with him and Gordon

112

told me. He hates Timbers as much as me, you see, so he tells me what ought to be said."

'As much as you,' thought the Chief Inspector. Yes, he probably does hate you that much. "You've been very helpful, Miss Tucker. I shall make sure that what ought to be said is put to good use."

* * *

Timberdick hid beneath the graveyard elm. She longed to be warm inside, rubbing herself in front of the vestry fire before she burrowed beneath the vicar's blankets. But she was too nervous of going to the vestry that night. Things were wrong – not seriously so, not enough for her to seek help or shelter, but uncanny co-incidences had put the night time out of sync. Stuart Morrison wasn't where he should have been. His father had tried to keep her from going out of doors. Ned Machray wasn't around; he wasn't at Goodladies Junction and not even in Jack's All Night Café. Timbers thought that the fat old copper should have been around in case things went wrong. Gordon Freya said that they must meet but wouldn't say why. And Sergeant Peacock – an unreliable and peculiar policeman – had followed her from one end of Goodladies Road to the other. Now, why would he do that? The trouble was in Timberdick's head, of course, it was nonsense to think that things had been set to trap her. Silly. What rubbish. It was the church in the dark that put her on edge.

She shivered in the cold and kept her coat close to her. Between the scurrying of the squirrels through the undergrowth and the squawking of crows high up in the trees, the steely blue clouds passed in front of the moon. (Blocking out the goodness, were they?) It made Timberdick picture a macabre night of magic in a Victorian drawing room, when a veil is held over the standard lamp and the guests grip fingers until the veil is withdrawn again.

But it wasn't just the night creatures that were alive in the graveyard at half past two. An old man with a sweater beneath his suit jacket and bottoms too big at the ends of his trousers, pushed his bike along the gravel path. He was taking a short cut to the railway footbridge. And, in the porch of a sunken door, a little door at the side of the church that was now so low in the ground that if it was

113

ever opened inwards, the turf and dirt would form an immediate step – a doorstep up from the threshold rather than down (something else that was wrong on this night for witchcraft) – here, two lovers got to grips. The boy played urgently, his hands working ahead of the pictures in his mind, but it was the girl who kept it all at high revs. She enjoyed the scamp and spank of fiery lovemaking. Calling for him to hurry, to hurt her, then biting his ear so that he had to break off. Pulling him towards her, then bending his fingers backwards and hurting him so much that he had to twist her hair in a knot to distract her. Ah! Yes! This was good jazz. And when it was over – her hair in a mess and damp – she marched down the church path, proudly, her crimson panties screwed in a ball in her hand. How many girls had carried their used up knickers out of this graveyard, Timbers joked with herself.

The man with the bike came back. A locked gate had barred his way through the railway fence.

The girl's bravado and exhibitionism shamed Timbers. Don't be a scaredy cat. She emerged from the darkness of the tree and walked around the church to the vestry door. Her footsteps crunching loudly on the loose stones as she walked. She was already fingering the iron key in her pocket when she reached the door. Should she hold her breath as she tried the lock? She held her tummy muscles tight, ready to cry out. She felt that her knees were ready to weaken. As soon as she got the door open, she put out a hand to switch on the light. When no-one spoke up, she walked into the room.

Someone had been here. The vestry had that Goldilocks feeling. A fire in the grate. Crumbs on an empty plate on the table. Who's been waiting in my vestry, said the little scared bear. Not I, laughed the ghosts in the roof of the nave, beyond. Nor I, whispered the wind between the tall stone pillars. Come here. Come and look, they said.

Silly, to check that the church was empty. It had passed two o'clock and she should have settled down at the vestry fire and burrowed beneath the vicar's blankets. Wasn't that all she had promised herself?

She listened to her footsteps. She walked slowly down the church aisle. Her high heels were loud on the slabs. Her skirt seemed much too short. Silly, she had stood on pavements for years in skirts much

114

shorter than this. Why should she feel so vulnerable here? But she did. The tops of her legs did. God, her bottom must almost be on show. On show for the church mice as they peeped from the cracks in the pews.

There was the font. Where innocent children were christened. And there was the hand. At the base of the font. Resting, like an artist would like to paint it. The fingers a little curled. The palm easy, making a little bowl to put a half crown in.

Timbers stood and watched.

Gordon Freya's body was crumpled behind the font with his left hand outstretched. There was something special about the way he was bending around the stone stump. As if he was trying to clutch at his infancy. The back of his head was open and brain oozed from the broken skull.

PART THREE

THE FUGITIVE

NINE

Spider's Web

The clock in the detention room had stopped three months ago and no-one had asked for it to be repaired. Time had no place in here. Peacock and Bloxham sat at one side of the bare, tubular framed table and Timbers, unconcerned, rested opposite. She kept a couple of feet away from the table; sideways on, her thin knock-kneed legs were stretched out. She slouched and she would have stuck her hands in her pockets, if she'd had any. She thought a policewoman should have been in the room, but Peacock and Bloxham said it was all right without one. No-one took notes. (There was no paper.) Peacock explained that they would write some questions and answers afterwards and, tomorrow, the typist in the Warrant Office would produce a statement for Timbers to sign. This way, the Warrant Office would make sure that the statement contained all the evidence required. "None of us are lawyers in here, are we?" said Peacock.

When he explained that Timberdick would have to spend a night in the cells because the Warrant Office typist wouldn't be in until the morning, Timbers shrugged her shoulders. It would be as comfortable as the vestry, she said. Not as warm but there wouldn't be the noises in the roof.

Peacock put the Yale key on the tabletop. "Won't you tell us what this is about?"

"Won't you tell me why I'm here? You know I didn't kill Mr Freya."

They had found the key when they took her valuables and put them in a brown envelop. Valuables? A cheap Timex, one of Rennie Tegg's Maltese lighters and a crucifix on a chain.

"We know you took the key from the body," Peacock said.

"Whose body? There are two of them now."

When Bloxham followed this with, 'What does the crucifix mean?' Peacock turned his head and said, "What do you mean, what does the crucifix mean?"

"I mean, does it mean she's got a faith?"

"Damn that," said Peacock quietly.

A policewoman knocked politely on the door and looked inside. "I'm looking for Chief Inspector Trent." She had black hair in curls and spoke in a clipped, slightly timid voice. She was the sort of girl who passed her eleven-plus, Timbers thought.

"Well, he's not here, is he?" snapped Peacock.

"Mrs Bellamy's at the desk and she wants to talk to him about you."

"Well, he's not here, is he?"

The policewoman dipped her head apologetically and left the room. When the door had closed, Timbers explained, "A kind old gentleman used to visit me. He'd recite passages from the Bible as he watched me undress. He liked me to wash in front of him, but he never touched me and always spoke nicely to me. When he called for the last time – and he said he wouldn't be coming again – he gave me the crucifix for a present."

"So it doesn't mean anything?" Bloxham asked.

Peacock queried, "About me? What's Mrs Bellamy got to say about me?"

"It means that I'm ready to be caught when God wants to catch me?"

Bloxham smiled. "It doesn't work like that."

"It does," said Timberdick. "God's got some catching up to do."

"No," persisted Bloxham. "It doesn't work like that."

"Look, leave it," the Sergeant said. "We're talking about the key."

Timbers yawned. "I'm tired. Can you lock me up now?"

"No we can't. Where did you get the key from?"

"You said you know. I got it from the body, you said." Then she sighed. "I thought it was the key to his lodgings, but it's not. It opens the front of McKinley's Curiosity Shop. Try it."

"So what was he doing with it?"

Timbers shrugged.

Peacock brought his fist down on the table. "Talk!"

"You want to beat her up, Serge?"

Peacock couldn't believe his ears. Again, he turned sideways. He said, "What did you say that for?"

"Ned Machray says you did it once in a bus shelter on the downs," the Detective Constable explained. "You beat up a prisoner, he says."

"God, Bloxham!" he shouted. "Get out of here!"

Bloxham stood up.

"You're not leaving me alone with him," Timbers declared. She pushed the chair onto its back legs and kept her balance long enough to push the alarm button on the wall.

Bells rang throughout the station and people shouted, "The cells! The cells!" Doors banged against walls as they were thrown open and heavy booted feet rushed along corridors and down stairs. A second bell started to sound in the front office and the ceiling lights flickered, as if they were on the point of fusing.

The policewoman was the first to rush into the room. "Oh, you've done it now," she crooned. "Ringing the alarm when you're in here with her. Just when Mrs Bellamy's saying awful things at the desk. Mr Peacock, she says you did awful things to Timberdick in the police car."

Then a large Sergeant pushed her out of the doorway and tried to grab Timbers. Bloxham moved to protect her. "It's not her! It's him!" he shouted.

"Him?" The Sergeant looked one way and leaned the other, asking too much of his balance. He slipped, ouching in pain as he went down on his ankle.

Bloxham threw himself backwards to avoid the tumbling Sergeant. He crashed into the table, collecting Timbers as he fell down. She felt unexpectedly safe in his arms. Bloxham kept hold of her, their eyes stayed together and, for a few moments, there was a ludicrous notion that they could suit each other.

"For God's Sake, will someone lock her up!" shouted Peacock.

* * *

121

Bernie Trent, cold but loosely satisfied, got back to the Tegg's place at four. Another hour, Rennie would be up and about, waiting for the first delivery of newspapers. The Chief Inspector kept quiet; he took off his damp coat and draped it over the banister post. (He meant to take it upstairs before the family came down.) He walked into the living room on his way to the kitchen. I was sitting in front of the fireplace without a light on. "There's been a leak," I said before he noticed me. I allowed him a few seconds to decide not to respond. "You were going to make yourself a pot of tea," I said. "If you switch the light on in the kitchen, we'll be able to see each other's face while we talk. Oh, don't worry about me." I gestured to the empty bowl on the hearth. "I've already had some soup."

It wasn't his place to ask what I was doing in Rennie and Do's living room but I could see that the matter bothered him. His craggy face with untidy grey hair and his sloping shoulders looked tired and low on patience. If he hadn't made an arrest that evening, bringing the murder case close to its resolution, he would have challenged my right to surprise him. He stood in the middle of the patterned carpet and said, "I'd rather talk to you in the dark, Constable." 'Constable' was intended to remind me that he was a Chief Inspector. Superior Officers are all the same, I reflected. Bloody superior.

"The Superintendent bumped into one of your colleagues this evening. Unfortunately, the chap thought our 'Super' was in on the secret and he gave away the best half of your little game."

"It's not my game," Trent said.

"The plan to convert an old aircraft carrier into a pirate radio ship and send it off to Rhodesia."

Trent said honestly, "It won't work in a million years but we were told to try."

"That's been your job from the beginning, hasn't it? This 'stolen cigarette case' was always a sideshow, an excuse to bring me back into the city. You knew that I'd get you close to people who are operating the radio pirate."

Trent stepped into the kitchen, found the kettle and started to make his tea. "It had to be done without a fuss. We didn't want to scare them off. We wanted to get alongside them."

"Do you know how hard I've worked to win the trust of people in this neighbourhood?"

"Really, we don't mean them any harm. They'll be no trouble."

My God, I thought. He still thinks I'm going to let him get away with it. I said, "Not this time. This time, you people aren't going to get what you want from me. Good Lord, do you think I'd let you involve folk round here in your shifty world of secrets and betrayal. I was your clockwork toy, wasn't I? A tinplate copper on a bicycle that you could wind up and let go. Who are you, Trent? I don't think you're even a policeman."

He preferred to be too busy to answer at once. "I have the powers of a constable, Constable," he said.

Bullshit.

"You know how it is." He was arranging items on a tray. Then, because he had run out of things to do until the kettle boiled, he came back into the living room.

"Smuggled cigarettes," I reasoned. "You're Customs and Excise, aren't you? No. No. You're a sailor. What are you? Some Under-Assistant Vice-Bloody Admiral?"

He sat himself low in an opposite chair. The light from the kitchen was behind him. "It doesn't matter what we are in our job, does it? That's why it works."

" 'Our' job? Don't include me."

"We 'do' things rather than 'be' things. That's why you've been part of it, Ned, and happily so. Ned Machray, you don't realise how highly valued you are. For twenty years you have been doing minor, 'running and fetching' jobs for the London Office, expecting no favours and causing no trouble. You are one of the reliable steadfast Sergeants who serve their country without praise."

"Except I'm not a Sergeant."

"It's time we put that right."

I said bugger off to that.

I heard Rennie moving about upstairs. I pulled myself to my feet and plodded off to deal with the waiting kettle. "Why are you holding, Timberdick? You know she didn't do the murder. She was talking to me on the phone when it was happening."

"She knows who the dead man is. I've always said that's the key to this case. We caught her next to Freya's body. That's enough to lock her up until she talks to us." When I carried the tea tray to the fireside, he said, "Keep away from her, Ned. I won't have you interfering. Not at this stage."

"Goodness sake, man. She knows who the killer is."

"What makes you so sure?"

"Because she's twice the detective you'll ever be. Let her go, Trent, and I'll make sure she gives you the murderer before this time tomorrow."

The Chief Inspector puckered his lips. "I can't do that," he said.

* * *

The Volunteer was my sanctuary. When I wanted to avoid the eyes on Goodladies Road or the noise of Chloed's Hoboken Arms, I would walk to the end of Rossington, cross the railway footbridge and follow the dog-walking alley to the side door of the Volunteer. It was a narrow-roomed pub with no music and no bar games except dominoes — not even darts because that encouraged people to stand up. Sometimes, Len would allow the British Forces Network to crackle and phut from a put-together rediffusion speaker in the corner. The Volunteer was a pub to smoke pipes in and the aroma of their favourite mix could identify each of the regulars. For years, Copley and Beetle called me 'Russian Ned' not only because I used Rennie Tegg's Russian rubbed tobacco, but also because of my socialist talk.

I took the walk slowly after my argument with Trent, and got to the pub shortly after nine. The place wasn't properly open, of course, and only George Copley was in. I collected the half a pint of mild that Len had poured without asking, and took it to my bar stool in the corner. I nodded at George and he went, 'Aye,' not very loudly. Maggie McKinley came in three minutes later; she had probably followed me from Tegg's place. Ladies were not allowed to buy their own drinks in the Volunteer (it was a rule that kept them out), so when Len put out a gin and tonic, he marked half on my slate and half on George's

"Do you want a lady to stand at the bar, Ned Machray, or will you escort her to a table?"

"What have you got to talk about, Maggie McKinley?"

"Important business."

I had known Maggie since the thirties when her two teenage tearaways were in all sorts of trouble and Bugger was treating her pretty badly. She battled on, making her own friends, helping folk and fighting their corners. A tough nut. But her lasting reputation was built beneath the German bombs when Mrs McKinley carried hot stew and baked potatoes to people in the streets. (In a city gallery, there's a picture of a woman doing this. The face isn't Maggie's, but the image can only have come from stories about her.) Now, people had a love for her, especially since old Bugger's death; only a grumpy old bear wouldn't spend a few minutes listening to her. "Sergeant Peacock's in trouble," she said. "Barbara Bellamy has told your Chief Inspector that the Sergeant took off Timberdick's bra in his patrol car and, before that, he had her hand up her skirt in my alley."

Good Grief. "Is she right?"

"Barbara thinks she is. She says that she saw the car from her shop window. Well, so did I and what I saw looked like Timbers' idea. Come on, Ned, you've been treated to an eyeful of Timberdick's topsiders."

I coughed uneasily and looked to my beer.

"Yes," she said, dealing with her own thoughts. "I've come to tell you that I told Barbara a man and a woman were in the alley and Barbara guessed I meant Peacock and Timbers. Except it wasn't. It was Gordon Freya and your Piggy Tucker."

Miss Tucker wasn't mine, I insisted.

"And it was an hour before the Walking Stick Man came."

I nodded, remembering that Piggy had told me she had been there. "She didn't mention Gordon Freya," I said.

"The upshot's for John Peacock," Maggie declared. "He's handed in his badge and 38."

I laughed. "We're not in New York, Maggie dear. We don't have badges or 38's. What on earth have you been reading?"

"Bernie Ohls," she confessed. "He's the best man in the D.A.'s office."

Grief.

"Do something about it, Ned Machray. Sergeant Peacock's been suspended and it's not his fault. He works hard and he's only young. He messed things up – I've heard all the tell-tales – but he's got most of the thinking right."

"He did mess things up," I emphasised.

"But he cleaned my kitchen, very nicely."

"He's arrested Timberdick and surely you don't think she murdered anyone."

"Of course, I don't." Maggie explained, "But it was Trent who told Peacock to pick her up and that was because of Piggy Tucker. Gordon Freya met Piggy at the dog track and told her what Shannelle had said. And Piggy went blabbering to Trent."

I hadn't known about Mo's part in Timberdick's arrest. I wiped the last of the beer from my lips.

"Jealousy, that's Piggy Tucker's crime," Maggie said, reading the anger on my face. "In the old days they used to put iron bridles in the mouths of women with naughty talk but, in all my years, I've found that there's only one way to deal with a jealous woman. Do you know what that is, Ned Machray?"

Widow McKinley wanted me to march off and deal with my miscreant lodger, but I had no belly for it. I wanted rid of Piggy Tucker, that's all. "Besides, it's Barbara Bellamy who needs to be taught a lesson. She should keep her lurid notions to herself. And when Timberdick gets hold of her – Heaven help the woman."

Maggie relished the prospect. "That's my way of thinking, Ned. The last time Timbers set about our haberdasher – perishing it was." She gathered her handbag and coat. "I can't spend hours drinking these days. Times were when I'd sit in the Hoboken and play hands of whist, between hot pot and dancing. Back in Lillie Horsepool's day. I'll leave matters in your hands, Edward." Usually, only women who didn't know me called me Edward. (My mother called me Edwin but I left that behind with my schooldays.)

After Maggie left, I returned to my bar stool and asked for whisky rather than mild. "Have you ever heard of Bernie Ohls?"

"He's the D.A.'s man in the Phillip Marlow books," Lennie explained. "I've got some upstairs, if you like."

"Phillip Marlow? The Big Sleep and stuff?"

"Yeah, and stuff."

I should have been worrying about Peacock cleaning Maggie's kitchen but my head couldn't get free of the widow in her front bedroom, reading private eye pulps while Timberdick Woodcock ran a brothel across the rest of the house. I decided that McKinley's was a shop full of curiosities.

*   *   *

When I got to the police station at twelve, Ruby Redinutt was on duty in the cells and Timbers was alone in the detention exercise area. She was sitting on the garden bench.

"Have you ever thought about the birds?" she asked.

I put aside jokes about the skirted or feathered varieties. I said simply, "Not thoughtfully."

"A sparrow was skipping around here. It came really close. It wasn't tame but it trusted me. I thought, we're like two civilisations, us and the birds, living side by side for thousands and thousands of years, and not hurting. Like, live and let live."

I didn't think that turkeys and chickens would agree, but she said they weren't real birds. No more than Penguin biscuits in chocolate.

"I suppose I'm like a bird, allowed to flutter around here for an hour before you lock me up again in my cage."

"They won't let you go, Timbers," I said. "I've told the Chief Inspector that you could solve the murder in twenty four hours but he won't listen. They know that you didn't kill Gordon Freya."

"I didn't kill the Walking Stick Man either, but Peacock still arrested me."

"What happened that evening, Timbs?" I asked.

"God, Ned. How many times have I been over this in my head? We got there – Layna, Shannelle and I – about half past nine. David, the Butcher's Boy, must have been waiting for us because he knocked on the back door as soon as I put the lamp in the window."

"The lamp?"

"The bicycle lamp. When the stew-house is open, I put it in the wire meshed window, next to the dish of stewed prunes."

"Yes. The stewed prunes. Why do you do that?"

127

"It doesn't matter."

"No, really. I'd like to know."

"It's not important."

"Even so, I'm interested."

"Ask Stuart. He knows what it means"

"Is it about the smell?"

"God, Ned!" she snapped. "Shut up about the prunes!"

"I'm sorry, Timbs. You were talking about when the Walking Stick Man came. You got there and David was waiting, you said. Did Widow McKinley let you in or do you have your own key?"

"Maggie was there – she hardly goes out these days – but I always let myself in through the back. So, it was Maggie McKinley in her front bedroom, Shannelle and I in the kitchen, and Layna and David upstairs."

"In the attic?"

"I didn't know that straight away. I thought they were in one of the bedrooms. It was only when Layna came down because of the cold that she mentioned David was tied up in the loft."

"Cold, was it?"

"Freezing, Shannelle wanted to go home, but I wouldn't let her. I knew that Gordon Freya would be watching the house and there'd have been trouble if he saw her coming out. He didn't want her for himself, but he didn't want others to have her. Man's trouble. Like bloody kids with toys, they are."

"And you saw him waiting?" I asked.

"David did. That's what he told our new Ruby, later." A sharper mind would have picked up on 'our new Ruby' but I gave it no attention at the time.

"So that's why he was at the Curiosity Shop on the night of the murder?"

"Don't be fooled, Ned. He was still out to cause trouble for Shannelle if he got chance."

I asked, "Do you think he saw the Walking Stick Man arrive?"

"I don't know. He didn't tell me that."

I drew breath. "Mrs McKinley saw me tonight in The Volunteer. She says that Barbara Bellamy saw Freya down the side alley with a woman."

Timbers nodded. "Aunt Em. We know that."

"No. Maggie McKinley says it was Piggy Tucker."

"I don't believe that," said Timbers.

"Could Piggy have got into the house?"

"When Layna and Shannie and I were downstairs?" she considered thoughtfully. "And David was in the attic? Yes, Piggy could have climbed on the shed roof and leaned across to the landing window."

"Tell me what happened when the Walking Stick Man came?"

Timbers gathered her thoughts. "He wanted Shannelle. He said that from the start. He thought that Shann was still Freya's woman and he wanted her because of that. To make Freya jealous. Angry, perhaps. I tried to protect her, but Shannelle agreed to go upstairs with him. Ned, she hated him; I could see it. I thought she was going to mess things up for him. You know, have the last laugh somehow. Layna followed after a few seconds; she took the knife with her so that she could fix the heater. That's when you started ringing and Mrs Mack started banging on the shop ceiling at about the same time. Then the girls came down the stairs together, shouting that the man was dead."

"Who was on the landing when he was killed?"

"Layna and Shannelle. David was tied up in the loft and Maggie was in her bedroom."

"No, Timbers. Maggie McKinley was in her bedroom after the murder had taken place. That's why she was banging on the ceiling. Could she have killed the Walking Stick Man and then ran into her room?"

"Yes," Timbers said.

"Without the girls seeing her?"

"Without Layna seeing, yes. I don't know about Shannie because I don't know what she was doing, just at that moment."

"Who was holding the knife after the murder?"

"Layna. Blood was everywhere. All over her hands and arms and down the front of her dress. That's why I said she had to get his keys."

"I don't understand that."

"He was out late at night, so he'd have the key to his lodgings. No landlady's going to stay up to one or two in the morning, just to let their guest in. And probably, he'd be carrying no identification. A man like that comes anonymously to the stew-house. So, the key would be our only way of finding out who he was."

I completed the story. "Somehow, Shannelle mentioned it to Gordon Freya. And he told Piggy Tucker, who reported it to Bernie Trent."

"That's how Peacock arrested me. Look, everyone's talking about what went on in Peacock's car that night. Me taking my top off and all. But there's more to him than that. He let Freya take Shannelle home without a word. God, Ned, she was the one who took The Walking Stick Man upstairs. And do you really think he released me because I let him paw me? No, Ned, there's got to be more to the man."

"The truth will come out," I said lamely.

She looked up at the Superintendent's window, four floors above us. "I won't be making a complaint. Your Super came down and asked if things were true, what Barbara Bellamy said. I said they were true, but probably my fault. He agreed. We said, what could a girl like me expect? He sat with me for twenty minutes or more, looking at the little sparrow. He wanted to feed it biscuits, I think, but he's not good at saying things, is he? He asked me if you were the father of my child."

"Grief, I hope you told him no."

"I said you could be."

"My God, Timbers! What did you say that for?"

"Because it's true. You could be. I haven't decided yet." She looked me straight in the face. "I'm going to need you around me, Ned. I'm not sure that I've got what it takes to be a mother."

"Of course, you have."

She said, "Working in the stew-house was good for me. When you work on the streets, everyone knows that you are at the bottom. Everyone can see you taking it from the dirty blokes. Indoors, was like a step up. I'd got off the streets, Ned. I was out of the rag and bone cart and into the junkyard. Is that it, Ned? Is that what I tell my child when he comes close to me, or when he's sick, or when he's looking for some sort of rules to make sense of things. I've nothing to give him, Ned."

I said, "Why did you solve the two murders? Because you cared.

Because you thought it was important to do something about the world we live in."

"Is that it? Sounds precious little to me," she said.

"No. Just precious."

* * *

I kept my appointment to see the Superintendent. His note said 'See Me' and a message pinned to my locker said that he meant 'This Afternoon at Two.' When I left the lift at the fifth floor, he came striding out of the gents having spent ten minutes rubbing the excess oil into his scalp. Still, the hair sticked up.

"Need to talk," he said, marching ahead. "Follow."

My Superintendent didn't know that he was close to tears and allowing trivialities to distract him from his greater worries. C.I.D. wouldn't do as he said. W.P.C.'s were doing much more than he said. And the Borough Watch Committee was going above his head. The Chief Constable was keeping an eye on the police district – he had let it be known – and the canteen ladies were asking who was going to move into the Super's chair. News that one awkward Police Constable (who had returned from the country only a few weeks before – returned to haunt him, he was sure) was famously broadcasting jazz music from a pirate radio ship seemed to be the last nail in the coffin.

But, that morning, a stick of hair refused to lie down. He had watered it and greased it, employing so much Brylcreem that it irritated his neck and stained his collar. As I trailed obediently to his office, I saw that the back of his collar was soaked and he was walking as if he had nasty bumps on his toes. "Pens," he said as he walked into his room. "Need to check. They must be the right way up in my tunic pocket. Otherwise, ink and everything. Sit down. No, don't." He stopped. He stood behind his desk and grasped it with both hands. He coughed and said, "Constable, how could you!"

"Ah, yes. The wireless programme. I need to explain."

"You are a filthy fellow! I've known that you cavort with tramps and trollops, but I never thought you would sully another policeman's wife."

131

"Ah, yes. There's that as well."

"The poor woman has begged me to send her and her husband far away from you. I'll do what I can." He tried to make his eyes look piercing, but they were too weighty with worry. "I hate you, Constable. You are a filthy fellow."

"I am, Sir?"

"Yes. A filthy, filthy fellow. Last year, I said you could no longer work in my division. Now, I mean to sack you."

A knock on the door, and a woman walked into the office without permission. She wore a straw boater with candy-striped ribbons and a summer dress of diamond shapes of different colours sewn together at home. The dress looked ready to fall apart. "Uncle Nevvie!" she shouted.

"Rowena!"

She looked at me and offered her hand. "I'm the Chief Constable's daughter and you can call me Wee-Wee."

I played along. I held her fingers in mine and kissed the back of her hand. She curtsied and let her eyelids come down with pretended modesty.

"You've heard from Daddy?" she said to Uncle Nevvie.

"I have not."

"He thinks it's a super idea. Super, it's a super idea, Super." She laughed alone at the silly joke. "I've told Daddy that the pirate radio show is a wonderful way of keeping in touch with the community. Daddy says no, but then he is a stuffy old so and so. So, Mr Ned is to cease his broadcasts, I'm afraid, but we will make the best use of this reputation and rapport. People trust him, you see, Uncle Nevvie."

"Daddy, I mean the Chief, says what?" Already, he wasn't liking it.

"Daddy says that Mr Ned is to direct a brand new Police Dance Orchestra. It's to be a full time job. No more walking the beat for Mr Ned! At first, Daddy agreed to promotion to Sergeant and nothing more. But I explained that while Sergeants do lead American Forces Orchestras, they do so from the pit. Because they can play. And Mr Ned, well, he can't play a thing. That's why he needs to be the Director rather than a leader and he must be a gazetted officer."

"Absolutely not!" roared the Superintendent. He began to smack

132

the back of his head, which puzzled Rowena because she hadn't noticed the stubborn stick of hair. "This Force gazettes down to Superintendent level and no further," he said firmly.

"Well, Daddy said yes if you said."

This time, he pressed his knuckles into the desktop and spluttered 'Absolutely not!' through his teeth.

"So." She wobbled her head playfully on her shoulders. "It's just Inspector Machray. Daddy said."

"Temporary," insisted the Superintendent.

Rowena reached for my hand again. "Come on, Inspector Machray. I'll show you your new home."

"Temporary," he repeated. His eyes were red and hurting and his face was twitching.

But Wee-Wee had finished talking to him. She smiled sweetly and asked me, "Do you know anyone who could turn one of the classrooms into a studio?"

The office door closed behind us and, as we walked down the corridor, I heard the Superintendent shouting, "Temporary! Temporary Inspector!"

"Don't worry about Uncle Nevvie," she said. "I'll talk to him. He used to bounce me on his knee, you know. The best thing now is to keep out of his way for a few minutes. My car's outside. You don't mind being a passenger in a bright orange sports job, do you? I say, Inspector Machray sounds rather good, doesn't it?" The lift arrived and we stepped inside. As soon as she pressed the button, bells started ringing. Rowena put her hands to her mouth "My God! What have I done!"

"It's the cells," I explained.

"No. It's Uncle Nevvie. He's gone completely loopy."

The lift stopped at the third floor and two Sergeants got in. "Spider's Web," they said together. The funny one said, "You'll need your bike, P.C. Machray."

"Inspector, actually," said Rowena, and the Sergeant replied that he was only a Sergeant.

The detention area was in chaos. A cleaner refused to stop the electric buffer and policemen were doing silly walks to avoid tripping over the lead. The Station Duty Officer was trying to mark names on a sketch plan of the area. The plan was on his clipboard and, so far, ran to more than twelve sheets that he couldn't manage. The Inspector kept shouting 'Spider's Web!' and two Constables were checking cells and running to and from a blackboard in the lobby area.

W.P.C. Redinutt was sitting crossed legged on the newly polished floor. She was in tears. "I couldn't help it," she said to me. "I don't know how it happened. One moment, she was talking to me nicely. She asked me to go to the toilet for some tissue paper and she followed me. And pushed me against the wall. And grabbed my keys. And she's gone, Ned. Gone."

Rowena offered no sympathy. "Yes, well, Inspector Machray's with me," she said. "Come on."

The real Inspector shouted 'Spiders Web!' at her, and then said, "Grief, Rowena. What are you doing here?"

"Inspector Machray," she explained. "He's with me." And she led me out to the car park.

TEN

Shooter's Grove

"Will they catch her?" asked the Chief Constable's daughter as she drove in first and second gears along the Nore Road. They were digging up the tarmac outside the Post Office and it was going to take us forty minutes to reach Shooter's Grove. We were stuck in traffic in an open top sportscar and everyone could see us. Mrs McKinley had opened her Curiosity Shop and was chatting with Trent in the porch. Barbara Bellamy waved at me from the opposite pavement. She couldn't believe that I was in a swish two-seater with an up-to-date dolly-girl.

"Don't be embarrassed, Edwin," said Rowena. "Enjoy it. Now, tell me how they are going to find your girlfriend."

"They will roll out maps of Goodladies and pin them on the wall." I delivered my explanation one step at a time. "They will describe how the district is three main roads crossed by back streets and rat runs. They will assign two constables to half a dozen roads and send them off to search."

"And they'll find her?"

I shook my head. "Timbers is in the nooks and crannies. And the nooks and crannies aren't on the map. The P.C.'s know that –and the Sergeants do – but they won't be given time to search them. You see, Rowena, the Governors always assume that the Bobbies want to get away with doing as little as possible. And damned right they are. So, they'll arrange the search so that everyone's kept busy. No-one will be allowed time for a smoke or a drink."

"Or time to search the nooks and crannies," she said.

"It's the flaw in city policing," I said. "Ned Machray's law, I call it. If you manage policemen, the system won't work. If you don't

135

manage them, the policemen won't work."

She smiled like a Chief Constable's daughter should.

"It is," I said, "Great fun."

"Yes. I've always said policemen were great fun. There's a joke about me. Have you heard it? I'm supposed to be sitting in a pub when I notice one of Daddy's policemen. I ask him what he wants to drink and he says 'Watneys' so I go and buy him a glass of beer, but what he really said was 'What Knees!'"

I said I hadn't heard it.

"I've a confession," the girl said.

"So have I."

"I don't know anything about jazz music. Uncle Bernie phoned me in bed and said that one of our best Constables was in trouble. I'm only too pleased to help. Gosh, I'm looking forward to working with you."

"This isn't right," I said quietly. "I'm not an Inspector and I don't fit in this car."

"Edwin, don't be embarrassed. Enjoy it."

That morning, I began my four years occupancy of Shooter's Grove. It was such a golden time that when I retired in 1969 I reflected that this house – not its people, not even the music – allowed me to look back on my police service with satisfaction. Here is not the moment to chronicle the history of the property but I love the place so much that I cannot avoid a mention of its past. A well-to-do family had built Shooter's Grove before the district was absorbed by the city. Gradually, the gardens, the orchards, the parkland and playgrounds (some people say that our municipal canoe lake had once been Grove property) were eaten away by the town's expansion. By the turn of the century, the house had become a preparatory school for boys. But not a successful one. It was requisitioned during the first war as a recuperation home. It stayed in public hands as secondary living quarters for city officials, including the Chief Constable of the small police force and the Prison Medical Officers. There was a great scandal at that time, drawing such venom from the church leaders that the place was handed to school governors again. This time, it was a school for daughters of gentlemen. (The new bursar could remember his happy boyhood in the prep school and was something to do with church administration at the time of the hand over.) In 1946, it fell into police hands and functioned as a training centre throughout the fifties. More or less. It was little used. In 1965, the Police Dance Orchestra did not need to dislodge any instructors or students; the place was empty. Only the blue and yellow sign survived to say that it was a School for Constables. It was a large square looking and anonymous house hidden by high hedges on the corner of a busy road. Many people alighted at the bus stop outside and hadn't time to notice it before they were swallowed up in the shopping precinct.

"I can't promise you the place for ever," Rowena warned as she untied the string on the front gate. "But while my father's the Chief, I'll make sure the band has a home here."

I told her that the A.C.C. Ops had decreed that the centre must remain in place because of a commitment to provide a dormitory of six beds in case of nuclear attack.

"What difference will that make?" she asked as we walked along the overgrown path. We could hear the emergency bells of police cars racing around the city. Timbers' escape had raised the hue and cry.

"Well," I said. "If the bomb goes off, no-one will be left to say that the A.C.C. was wrong. Come on, I'll show you the kitchen. I bet there's tea."

When Rowena and I stepped inside, I knew I could make Shooter's Grove my own. It had no carpets or curtains and only a few pieces of office furniture. But, I counted excitedly, three staircases, a fireplace in every room and roses in relief around every light. I wanted to check that the bath still had great brass taps.

The telephone was ringing when I reached the Inspector's office. "Do you have any officers? Any Constables-under-Training?" asked the old sweat in the radio control room.

"Not at all."

"This is Spider's Web. A prisoner has escaped from Central. We're activating Spider's Web."

I pulled a face.

"Spider's Web, do you hear? All available staff to muster."

"Not here," I said and put the phone down.

I heard crockery rattling down the corridor and guessed that the

Chief's daughter was busy with the tea. But I was wrong. Rowena was looking through a window at the unruly back garden. "It's a jungle," she called out. Moments later, Piggy Tucker carried the tea tray into my office.

"Get out!"

Piggy stood still. "Neddie, don't be cross. Timbers said." Her eyes were sad like a spaniel's and her mouth was down at the corners.

"Get out!" I repeated.

But Rowena was standing behind her and the look on her face told me that Piggy would be staying. "Timberdick thinks that Maureen's had such a horrid time, this week. She suggested that she should be your cleaner." She said firmly, "I agree."

"Where will she be sleeping?" I asked

"Edwin!" exclaimed my new patron.

"At the dog track," Piggy promptly assured me. "I'll sleep in the greyhound toilets."

"Oh, Edwin. How can you allow that?" said Rowena, very softly and kind.

"But she got Timbers locked up."

"But Timbers says she can work here."

"She did," Piggy reinforced. "Timbers said."

Timbers said. Of course, she did.

ELEVEN

On the Run

Do you remember when you were twelve or thirteen, Timberdick, and you were running from the pig man and the bunker of grass cuttings was the only place to hide? It was dark in there; so black that you couldn't see, no matter how wide you opened your gobstopper eyes. The cuttings got up your nose and in your mouth and they made your eyes sting. And you couldn't wave the midges away because you were too scared to move.

It's the same now, Timbers, except that you are in the coal shed at the back of Mrs Pitt's house. And it's coal dust that you can taste in your mouth and feel in your eyes. And the coal flies are fiercer than the midges. They are long bodied and steely and come at you like darts from nowhere. You could swear that they have jaws or claws on their heads that keep nipping you.

Terry Morrison tells you to pay attention. You try. You want to. But you can't see him in the dark. Is he the pig man, Timbers? How many times have you said it? Only a bad man comes fishing in a mucky pool like yours.

Timbers rubbed her eyes and listened hard.

"Do as you're told," Morrison said. "These people are well paid but they are risking a lot for you. If you don't stick to what we've agreed, they could end up in prison and they won't help the next guy."

"How much will it cost, Terry? I've got no money."

"Don't worry about that."

"Terry, I can't pay."

"Listen. If you're caught, you won't have to pay. If you get away, you have all of your life to think about it. Besides, my lad's just lost

139

his mother. I'm not going to let him lose his best friend."

There was silence between them and Morrison hoped that she wasn't going to offer herself on a bed.

"Thank you," she said meekly. "Tell me what to do."

"I'm going to hide you in the back of a car. Don't talk to the driver. I can't come with you but, Timbers, you mustn't try to identify the bloke behind the wheel. Keep your head down. No looking. No talking."

Timbers nodded obediently.

"Lay down, but picture where he's taking you. Through the dray yard of the Rifleman and along the alley towards Crowhurst Street. He'll drive slowly because the alley is only just wide enough for his car. At the top of the alley, he'll stop as if he's looking both ways before pulling out. He's waiting for you to bail out. Out through the right-hand door, Timbers. That's the one behind the driver. You'll fall straight through the wooden gate at the side of a house. Don't knock. The people are expecting you, so the back door will be open. Go straight in and straight upstairs. It will be about eight, so the family will be watching television. A big woman – as big as a ship – and her husband and their daughter. Don't introduce yourself. They don't want to see you. Make a noise as you go upstairs so they'll know you're in. Go straight to the front bedroom. It's the door at the top of the stairs. Shut yourself in and don't come out until I fetch you. Not at all. Not even for nature."

"Not even for nature?"

"Look under the bed, Timbers. You'll manage."

"Can I put the light on?" she joked. "Will that be all right?"

"Timbers, do exactly as this family wants."

"Yes, Terence."

"I'll pick you up on Sunday night. By that time, I'll have arranged to get you out of the city."

"No. I can't wait that long. I want you to hide me until Friday evening. That's all. Then, I've got to put this murder right."

"You're crazy."

"I've got to do it," Timbers insisted.

"O.K. But only if you let me help you."

Now, Timbers took the lead. "Stuart's got to tell Ned Machray

140

about Friday's drop. He's to give away all the details—but the wrong place. Trent has got to be at the wrong place at the right time. Now this is important, Terry, the lad's got to speak to Ned in the back garden of Shooter's Grove. Otherwise, my plan won't work."

"You're mad. You'll end up in prison."

"And, I've got to get a message to Chief Inspector Trent."

"Well, you can't."

"Stuart can. Say, Shannelle's in danger and Trent's got to protect her."

Timbers left the coal shed as darkness fell across the city. The old Velox engine kept churning as she climbed into the back of the car and crouched her little body on the floor. The dust and grit from the rugs mixed with the exhaust fumes that came up through the decayed chassis. She was coughing and spluttering as the car crawled along the Rifleman's alley. The car stopped, its engine still chugging noisily in the night, and Timbers extricated herself but, fearing that she might be sick, she leaned against the wooden fence for two minutes before entering the house.

Terry had been right. The television was on and Timbers heard the family unwrapping sweets. She stamped up the stairs and didn't pause until she was inside the bedroom. Was she supposed to switch on the light? What had Terry said? It was nonsense that she could live for two days without electric light. She took off her shoes and walked in stockings to the curtains. Could she do this? Could she risk drawing the curtains open? She stepped to the side of the window and tugged, very carefully, at the curtain hem. Little enough to let in the light from the streetlamps. Then she sat on the floor at the foot of the bed and tried to make sense of her surroundings. A bed with a tall headboard and plenty of blankets. An old eiderdown that didn't fit. A light switch on a string, hanging from the ceiling. Two pictures on the walls but it was too dark to see their subjects. An armchair. A hard chair. And a footstool that Timbers decided to sit on. She put her head in her hands; all this meant nothing. Even the address on the corner of Crowhurst Street – a street she had walked many times – meant nothing. Where was the value of knowing where she was if she wasn't allowed to touch the truth of it? Talk to no-one, hide from everything and there is nothing here to touch.

She allowed curiosity to draw her away from her mood. She reached beneath the bed. Yes, just as Terry had promised, the chamber pot was there. She got herself to giggle about it. Then she climbed on to the bed and settled with her knees drawn up to the chin. Sitting in this way in the dark, she went over her plans for the next two days. Everything relied on her guess that young Stuart had borrowed a mucky book from the old vestry. Yet, oh God, she had forgotten to tell Terry that the boy must bring it to her.

The family was bedding down for the night. Timbers listened to the to-ing and fro-ing. Water running in the bathroom. The shouts of Goodnight. (Timbers worked out that it should have been called four times.) The opening and closing of doors. The last person climbing the staircase to bed.

Timbers went to the window and, more confident now, looked over the rooftops, down to the tips of the dockyard cranes three or four miles away. She didn't want to go to bed. She didn't want to undress in this room. She didn't want to close her eyes or take her mind off things. She looked down at the pavements and wanted to see someone she knew, but there was only a man smoking a cigarette on the street corner.

After an hour's quiet, the bedroom door opened and the woman of the house walked in. As big as a ship, Terry had said. She was in her fifties and had a farmer's shoulders and the fists of a prize-fighter. Her forearms were muscled and came forward like the claws of a crab in science fiction. Her face was square. She had hair on her lips and tufts on the proudest edges of her cheeks. Her jaws and chin looked as rough as sand. Sand in concrete, that is. She was carrying supper – things in gravy on a plate- and, as she approached, Timbers caught the stale smell of her body.

"Some hotpot, dear."

Timbers said, "Thank you," but thought, 'God, this woman sounds like something bad in a fairy tale.'

"No dear. You eat it while it's hot. You must be famished."

"Please, before you leave," Timbers said. "I need you to help me. I need St Mary's Curate to come and see me."

"Are you troubled?" the woman asked.

"No, but I need to see him. I know that it's dangerous for you but

142

I promise that he will not tell people I'm here. Perhaps, if you bring him to see me at five o'clock tomorrow and I leave straightaway? Then even if he does tell the police, they'll find nothing here."

"How old are you?" The old woman's teeth were uneven and chipped.

"Thirty-five," Timbers replied, telling the truth.

"Then you'll want the old Vicar."

"No. You see, we can trust the Curate. He knows that I've been living in the vestry and he's told no-one. He knows that I found the keys to the church, years ago, and he's told no-one."

"I see," said the woman as she left the room.

Left alone, Timbers pulled the armchair to the window so that she could eat the hotpot in the light from the street. If Timbers' mother had been rich and if she had sent Timbers to a boarding school, it would have felt like this. Banned from the dining room and made to eat her supper alone in the dormitory. Without the light on. When she was sure that the woman wasn't coming back, Timbers opened the bedroom door, just enough, and laid the empty plate on the carpet outside. Then she took off her clothes and climbed into bed. She lay so that she could open her eyes and see the orange lights across the city, her back to the door.

She was ready to sleep when the bedroom door opened and the bedclothes were drawn away. Timbers felt a nylon nightdress against her body as the old woman climbed onto the mattress. The big ship coming to berth Timbers thought. The woman lay down on her side – her front against Timbers' back – and her strong arms reached around Timbers' waist and chest. Timbers pushed herself into the warm, smelling flesh. A grandma's sweat. A washerwoman's cuddles, the powdered-over coarseness of a fat woman undressed. Timbers knew that, if she asked, this woman would be patient with her.

"You'll want to know what I've done," Timbers said.

"You're a prostitute, dear. You're expecting and you've been locked up on a word of a friend. You've no place to go. You've been sleeping in the church for three weeks. And you've been looking out for young Stuart Morrison.

"Terry's told you all this?"

"Terry's told me none of it. He thinks it's better for me to take in a stranger and know nothing about her. He also thinks I'm a fool. Now go to sleep, my dear."

"The Curate?"

"He will be here at ten o'clock tomorrow. Now, no more talking; you're spoiling things."

A powerful hand took hold of Timbers' breast and pulled it hard.

* * *

Sunshine and cricket woke Timbers at eight-thirty. Crowhurst Street had a dead end so the children could play without too much interruption from cars. The house was quiet and Timberdick guessed that the husband had already left for work and Annie had not returned from the early shops. "Stay put until ten, Duck," the older woman had said, before dawn, when she lolloped out of bed like a blubbery walrus.

Timbers dressed in yesterday's clothes. Sure that the house was empty, she saw no harm in using the bathroom. She didn't know if it was still out of bounds; had the night with old Annie changed the rules?

The two women had slept warmly, without lovemaking, but with an easy togetherness that looked for no words between them. Timbers disturbed only once, when Annie found room to smack her bottom. "Up you get, Duck. You're fidgeting for the toilet. Off you go now." Timbers returned with the chamber pot on her mind. How was she supposed to use it? If she sat on it, she would break the porcelain. To squat over it was trusting too much to luck.

"Am I supposed to stand with my legs apart and hold the pot with my hands? No, no, I've got it. You want me to stand at ease, put the pot in place and keep it there by pressing with my thighs."

"Go to sleep now," said Annie. She wanted nothing to do with Timbers' invitation to be rude.

At nine o'clock in the morning, Timbers was sitting on top of the staircase when she heard the front door open. "You've got to move on," Annie called from the passage. "Someone's been asking questions about you. She knows you're here."

"Who? Annie, what about the Curate?"

"You don't know my name! You forget it, my woman."

"No, Annie." Timbers was half way down the stairs and talking urgently. "Annie, I've got to see the Curate before I go."

"You go now!"

"But you were going to tell me about Terry. How long have you known him? What should I know about him?"

"You've got to go, dear, at once."

"The Curate?" Timbers pleaded. "You said he was coming at ten. Last night, you said."

"Where shall I send him on to?"

Timbers hesitated. She couldn't promise to be anywhere. Even if she knew where she was going, she would have been foolish to arrange a rendezvous that might prompt her arrest. But, she argued with herself, she was dealing with two people she trusted. Say any time, Timbers. Say any place and be there.

"I can't say," she said. "Tell him—"

"Tell him what?"

Timbers' chewed her bottom lip. "Tell him that I need him to let some tyres down. Tell him to be on the beach by the yacht club at midnight. He'll see a van on the shingle. A brown van with two windows at the front. I'll be there but he mustn't speak to me. He must wait until I've drawn the driver away, then he must let the tyres down."

"Let the tyres down?" queried the housewife. "Will a Curate do that?"

"Tell him it's for the sake of a child."

Timbers had no packing to do. She had no handbag or coat to collect. Thrown onto the risky streets, Billie Elizabeth 'Timberdick' Woodcock turned her face against the hiding places. Little rooms in the houses of friends, tarpaulins on the backs of lorries, sheds and privies in unknown yards – they all courted discovery, arrest and gaol for life. She had to stay free until the next day's dawn yet, because her spindly figure and cork-like face was so well known on the pavements and in the doorways, she knew that she would be recognised. To stay hidden she would have to be lucky and girls like Timbers couldn't count on eighteen hours of luck. She knew that she would be seen and reported, so Timbers had to keep moving, so that all trace of her would be gone when the posse turned up.

At eleven o'clock, (had she been on her toes for only one hour?) she was sitting on bricks in a builder's yard when the workman came out with a mug of tea. He sat and talked, making much of the cement dust on his face and the state of his dungarees, and only let on at the end of his tea break that he knew Timbers was on the run. "You come back, girl, after the place is closed. I'll let the man with guard dogs know."

Timbers moved on, hesitating at corners and staying back from road junctions. In her quiet loneliness, she let her mind wander through all that she knew about the places. The archways and yards – where working people had plied their trades before the First World War. And the broken garages where, even if they did look more like livery stables than engineering shops, young men had tried to develop their motor businesses in the twenties and thirties. Repairing one car, building a second and no room for a third. There had been as many as twelve different garages, though none lasted more than two years. Now, they were just names in old street directories and all the heartache meant nothing. She passed the scrub where Mrs Pitt had been trying to grow vegetables for eight years, at least. Twenty years before her, ginger-faced Derek Caxton had operated a motorcycle courier service from the same patch of earth. A parcel-taxi, he had called it. (He didn't come back in 1940.) Timbers had heard all the stories so many times that they had become part of her tapestry. She believed not only the stories but also what the stories said about her neighbourhood.[4]

Then, there were the scarred places where murders had been played out. Seven bodies in eighty years and three of them known to little Timberdick. Today, she hurried past Smithers Garage, where I had found Layna Martins beaten and raped, and the Methodist porch, where pretty Yvonne Young and her Polish obsessive had ended up dead. How safe were they now, these streets that she owned so well

---

[4]Now, forty years later, Timberdick has become part of the folklore. The Hoboken Arms has gone, along with Smithers Motor Garage and the stone porch to the Methodist rooms. But the people recall the skinny prostitute, old before her time, who waited on the pavements. Little is made of her detective work, while her reputation for caring for the other girls is exaggerated.

and where she had lived and worked for twenty years?

She didn't run but developed a sense of pace, going from back shed to side alley, from rooftop to stairwell, and always knowing when she had been too long in one place. But it was difficult to keep away from people.

When she crept into the back of the newsagent on the Nore Road, wanting to take a cup of water from the kitchen sink, she heard Ruby's voice in the front shop.

"He didn't know that it was being broadcast," she explained to the other women. "Ned thought that he was just recording some songs for Sean, that's all."

"So how did he get out to the pirate ship?"

"He didn't," Ruby persisted. "He was on a tape that they played."

"Well, I think he was very good at it. Good enough for the BBC, I say."

It was some minutes before Timbers could catch Ruby's attention. The two girls huddled in the passage between the kitchen and the shop. "Did you get into trouble?" Timbers whispered.

"No. They don't know that I helped you. They were so bloody ready to assume that I'm useless that they didn't ask me any questions. Not really. Look, we shouldn't be seen together." The W.P.C. seemed very pleased with herself. In a perverse way, she thought that she had achieved something. Allowing Timbers to escape.

"I want to help you, Ruby. I want to thank you."

"Please, call me Dorothy Rose. I don't want to be Ruby any more."

"Listen, you can have the arrests. I can help you arrest the whole cigarette smuggling gang."

The policewoman took Timbers' arm and pushed her against the wall. "You know who they are?" she asked incredulously.

"No, but I know where they are going to be tonight. A large stack is being dumped on the shoreline after midnight and the gang's going to pick it up."

"Who told you this?"

"Ned's grass, but you mustn't say."

"And where? Where is it going to happen?"

TWELVE

Shore Patrols

There is a blues song that says whatever we do today won't matter in a hundred years. So, throw your kisses around, it says, who cares? (It doesn't mean just kisses, of course.) If the highbrows tell us that making a million pounds now won't be rewarded with immortality, then why should loose morals bring on eternal damnation? That's the drift of the song. And Timbers had stood on so many street corners that she believed the sermon. Every last comma of it.

It was half past nine, still early, but it was wet and cold so it felt like a long night. Timbers' thighs were damp where the drizzle got between the tops of her stockings and the hem of her miniskirt, and the biting wind was starting to ice things up. One of the girls had left a parcel of clothes beneath the concrete bench in the Methodist porch, trusting that Timbers would find them. She had an orange bomber jacket, orange high heels and her fishnet nylons. Chocolate and 12/6d were tucked in the jacket pocket. Timbers had been leaning against the white stone wall of the Yacht Club pavilion for forty-five minutes. No-one came this way.

Across the road, the gravel beach rose to a ridge, capped with clumps of rough grass, and beyond was the sound of the tide in the estuary. If the night had been warmer, she would have walked to the water's edge and tried to catch an idea of what was happening further along the coast.

Jack's van turned up on time. He drove slowly along the foreshore, checking that no-one was about, and then returned to the hard standing, next to the lifeboat station's toilets. He turned off his engine and waited.

Timberdick dawdled across to him. "I'm supposed to rob you," she said. Jack wound the window down.

The idea was nonsense, but Jack played along. "Oh yes, Timbers? What have I ever done to you?"

"It's not you, is it? It's the Duty Free that you're picking up."

"Christ, you know about that?" he exclaimed.

"I'm supposed to nick your van and take it up to the rendezvous. Then the others will load up instead of you."

"Now, how are you going to pinch this van off me?"

She tried to look cute. "I could make it worth your while."

He laughed at her. "You've picked the wrong Jack, my pet. I'm the guy who won't let you into his café when it's snowing outside and it's so cold that your butt gets stuck to the drainpipe, remember?"

There had been a time, pretty much like that.

"So you'll not be seducing me, Timberdick Woodcock. You and the other girls irritate my bones to rattling. Running up and down the alley like whippets, I've always said."

"Ah, you're a man's man," Timbers responded; the driver wasn't sure if she was making fun of him. "No, I mean it. I've always said that Jack in The Café would give more to a woman than he'd take. Not interested in Timbers, that's Jack. I guess, a woman like me would offer you nothing worth taking."

Jack agreed. Except for her blonde hair, he thought. It was short like a boy's and feathery in a way that made him want to run his hands through its tufts. It made her head look sexy. Not her face. God, that was comic – but there would be something good about holding Timbers by the back of her head. He kept his thoughts to himself.

"I need someone to walk with me, Jack. I'm cold and fed up and this night's going to finish me off."

"I've told you. You're not going to trick me."

Treat your men like dogs on leads. That's how Timbers had taught Shannelle to pull a man. Imagine he's on a length of string. If he wants something, tug the string tighter and make him walk towards you. He asks you a question? Well, take two steps back and answer softly. He'll come forward if he wants your reply. Say something nice, but make him take another step before he can hear it

149

properly. Make sure he knows you want nothing from him; tell him again and again. But when he looks for something from you, just a smile or a word or a bit of praise, he's got to get out from behind the wheel; he's got to walk into the shadows, then he's got to touch you. And touch you up close. And don't forget, once he's touched you in a way that his mother wouldn't like – he's caught. There's no going back or you'll tell on him.

Timbers thought that she was better than any of the girls at this. She talked more, but more softly and she kept her distance. At first, he kept saying 'pardon' (a little too irritably; be careful, Timberdick) and he leaned through his open window. Then, with only a little more conditioning, he got out of the van. (She'd won and she knew it. It would take time, probably more time than usual, but Timberdick knew that the big man would not be getting back into his van until she had finished with him.)

"Look, Timbers," he said as they walked behind the locked toilet block. "I didn't even want this job. You know me; I'd never normally get involved, would I? I sit behind the café counter and let the world go by. Isn't that the Jack you know? But I owe money, you see. Listen, I can't let you do it. You can't take the van off me, just like that."

* * *

Three miles away, a Regulator was watching a launch through binoculars. "We're in business, Sir," he said to the duffle-coated detective, behind him.

Trent had been sulking for an hour or more. He had doubted the information from the start and, with every set of lights that sailed innocently past, his disappointment deepened. "We're in the wrong place," he responded bitterly to the shore patrol. "We've been tricked."

Every so often, a fishing boat would speed up, then take us for a harbourmaster's post and turn tail, disappearing into the night. "We'd do better chasing them than sitting here," Trent grumbled.

Suddenly, he barked, "P.C. Machray! How long are we supposed to stop here?"

I climbed down from the Land Rover and walked towards him, when the Regulator with the glass perked up. "A boat's coming in. It's ours, Sir. Definitely!"

"Do you want us to deploy the shore patrol?" I asked.

"Not yet, Ned."

"Blast! She's waiting offshore."

He walked down the slipway until the water was just missing his toes. He kept his hands in his pockets and hunched his shoulders against the damp and cold. He stared at the lights at sea and tried to make sense of the sound of chains being drawn across steel, far off. He looked lonely and defeated, but he was a professional who knew that some jobs worked out and others didn't. I wondered what else he had in his life. He hadn't mentioned a family. He didn't seem to have a home. Eight months before, he had sat in the corner of the New Forest inn and made me step across the room to him. Now, I felt that same draw as I wandered to the water's edge.

"Do you like this place?"

"I can't live away from it," I admitted.

"It's muck," he said. He flicked his toe at a knot of mud and seaweed. Then he noticed that his socks were wet. He clenched his fists. "You were right, Ned. They've set your woman up, just as you said."

"She's not my woman, Sir," I said quickly and only to get the facts right.

"The informer made sure that she got hold of duff information. That's why we're sat here, on the wrong side of the harbour and three miles up the wrong creek."

I said – carefully, because I didn't want to cross the Governor. "I thought the information was wrong. Young Stuart had the wrong look about him. That's why I didn't pass it on."

"But he knew that your Miss Tucker would be listening," said the Chief Inspector. "And he knew that she'd report it to me."

We both knew that the deception wasn't Stuart's idea.

"I'd like to give them a run for their money, Sir," encouraged the Regulator.

Chief Inspector Trent wrapped his raincoat around his body. "No, we'll call it off," he said.

* * *

After eight minutes – and Timbers almost counted them in her head –
Timbers emerged with Jack from behind the toilets.

"It's still here, Timbers," Jack exclaimed. "Lord, I wasn't
expecting it. I was so sure you'd suckered me. All the time we were
doing things back there, I was saying in my head, 'She's fixed
something to happen. The van won't be there.' Hey, is this my lucky
night or not? I can't believe it."

Timbers felt crushed. The Curate had not played in his part in her
plan. Now, she could not prevent Terry Morrison's taking delivery
of the stolen cigarettes or the arrests that would follow. "I was
supposed to distract you while somebody let the tyres down,"
Timbers conceded. "It seems to have gone wrong."

"Ah! But you didn't distract me." He bubbled with excitement. "I
argued. You see, I suggested walking behind the toilets and you said
yes. That's not distracting me. That's –that's cheating and cheats
never prosper!"

"It's not a game, Jack."

"You've lost," he announced and climbed into the driver's seat.

Sunken shoulders and head down, Timbers walked across the
shingle to the narrow harbour road. She didn't look. Ahead, was a
four-mile walk in the cold and the dark, back to the city. She had
plenty of time to contemplate her failure. She heard him try to start
the engine, two or three times, but thought nothing of it until Annie
emerged from the bushes at the side of the road.

"He won't get it going," she said. She offered the small part that
she had extracted from the engine. "I couldn't convince the Curate.
No, I'll be honest. I didn't try. I wanted to be part of the prank,
Timmies. I have so little fun these days."

Jack was out of his van and shouting at them. "You've made a fool
of me. They'll string me up when they hear that I've lost the Duty
Frees."

Timbers called back, "I won't tell."

"One day, you will. One day, you'll say Old Jack's a duffer." He
ran forward but gave up after only a few yards. "What have you
got?" He shook his fist like an angry farmer. "Have you got anything

152

of mine, you'll show people? 'Look here, that was Old Jack on the night I made a fool of him.' A photo? You've taken a photograph of me. That woman who broke the van, she'll have taken the photograph."

But Timbers and Annie were already through the yacht club fence and looking for an open window. "I need to get to a phone," Timbers said.

"I've a car, Timmy. I'll run you back to town."

* * *

For eight months, Dorothy Rose 'Ruby' Redinutt had successfully spied on each delivery of cigarettes. She had found a hiding place, just twenty yards from the beach but safely concealed, from where she could check that the men did what she had told them to do. But tonight, there was no job. The two men waited for a launch that didn't arrive and a van that was stuck three miles away. When Dorothy Rose was sure that no other policemen were about, she walked quietly down to the shore. "The job's off," she said sadly. "It's too risky to go ahead. They don't know who we are, but they've got the time and the place right. So, I cancelled the drop."

The older of the two men wiped a hand over his damp face. "It's the bloody kid, isn't it?"

"You mean the Morrison boy."

"I mean the girl. Bloody Timbers-what's-it."

Dorothy Rose told them it was time to get clear. "We'll give it a rest for a year. We've done well. Next Christmas, we'll do even better."

THIRTEEN

Timberdick Closes the Case

Timberdick was standing alone in a cobbled square between the old Garrison Church and a row of weather-beaten seafront flats. "Stuart? Is that you?" As she spoke, Timbers fixed her eyes on the street corner and tried to make herself smaller in the phone box.

"Has Dad been arrested?"

"No," she assured the lad. "Nothing like that. I can't tell you what's happened but I need your help. It's important." An Austin Mini parked against the opposite kerb; its headlights died. "I'm counting on you, Stuart."

"I won't let you down, Mum."

Timbers smiled but let the boy's slip of the tongue pass by. "I need you to get a message to Ned Machray, but I'll get pinched if I contact the police station. So you've got to do it for me. Phone the front desk, say Ned's got to meet you outside Rennie Tegg's in half an hour. You not me."

"Shit."

Timbers frowned. Why was he using bad language again? Was he trying to warn her? Was somebody with him? "Stuart, it's not you he's meeting. It's me. But you mustn't tell anyone. Don't let any policemen know I'm involved. If you do, they'll put me in gaol." A light went on, upstairs in a house, and Timbers twisted her body to look. "So, don't tell anyone it's me. Not even, Ned." When the boy didn't reply at once, she added, "Stuart, is anybody there, listening to you?"

"But shit, Timbers. The new D.C.I. lives with Mr and Mrs Tegg. He'll see you."

"Stuart, don't use dirty words like 'shit'. It's not nice." She could hardly believe it; she was sounding more mother-like than Joyce Grenfell.

"I'm sorry."

"No, you're a good boy. I wouldn't be asking you to do this if you weren't a good boy."

"That makes me sound like a dog," he mumbled.

A young woman came out of the flats, swinging a white shoulder bag. Timbers watched anxiously as the dolly bird trotted around the mini and angled herself – stupidly trying to conceal her Pretty Polly legs – into the front passenger seat. The headlights caught Timbers as the little car turned in the road. She tried to hide – but then told herself off for being so nervous. It was nothing. A boy and his girlfriend going off together, that's all.

Timbers was still bothered by Stuart's doubts. "You're his grass, Stuart? How do you usually get in touch?"

He hesitated. (I had told him not to tell.) "When I can't reach him – and only when it's urgent –"

"Yes."

"I ring the lady who does our school crossing. She knows him."

"Christ," whispered Timbers. "Bloody-awful-Jennie."

"Leave it to me, Timbers. I won't let you down."

"Listen." She wanted to make this clear. "You've got to give Ned the book you found in the vestry. The one with the dirty drawings in it."

"Bloody hell, Timbers. How did you find out about that? Look, I was only–"

"Yes, I know what you were only doing, young man. Just give it to Ned."

"Dad says you're having a baby."

"Don't worry about that now. Ned's got to bring the book of drawings."

"I won't let you down, Timbers."

She told him she loved him.

"And Timbers, I'm sorry about taking the book."

* * *

Rennie Tegg was working late in his shop. The yellow light spilled onto the pavement and Radio Luxembourg competed with an ITV film from a back room. When old Mr Berkeley rapped on the shop window, Tegg unlocked the door. Berkeley wore a cloth cap, an old suit jacket and woollen mittens. Recently, he had taken to putting bicycle clips on the ends of his trousers, although he never rode a bike. He was always telling people that he hated women, but sometimes he offered Timbers a few shillings; she always turned him down.

Timberdick leaned against a wet drainpipe where a side road joined the other side of the street, a few yards up. The drainpipe ran from leaky guttering above two garage doors. It was a good place because there were no windows and the corner streetlamp wasn't usually working. The council used to repair the light, every month or so, but someone always took it out again. Kids, or one of the girls or blokes who wanted a dark spot on their way home from the pubs. Now, it was as if the Highways Department understood that the locals wanted the light out.

Timbers stayed still and watched.

She heard Tegg say, "We're not really open."

"Well, you're making enough noise, you ought t'be. What's going on?"

"Our Cherry's in a mood. She thinks her mum and I will go out if she blasts the tele. So, I thought I'd set up in competition with the portable radio in here."

"Bloody nonsense," said Berkeley. "Bloody childish. Have you got any dry tailor-mades?"

The Milky Bar song had started on the radio. "These new adverts aren't as good as the old ones," Tegg remarked as he looked beneath the counter.

"No – oo," Berkeley agreed.

Tegg sang, "It's the only way to see … what's coming on ITV … so run and get the TV Times."

"Ye-es," said Berkeley. "That's an old one, all right. Have you heard our Ned on the radio?"

"Our Ned? A radio star?"

"He's a pirate. He's playing his jazz records on the pirate radio ship, one night a week, that's all. Him and young Sean from the red record shop. I'm surprised you don't listen to our very own pirate

156

radio ship, Mr Tegg; it's better than Caroline, the young 'uns say, though I've never heard that one, myself. And I know it's better than your Luxembourg. Better adverts, too. 'It's the only way to see ... what's coming on ITV.' Ned's Jazz Records on Tuesday nights. Don't miss it, Mr Tegg" He left with a packet full of loose cigarettes that Tegg sold cheap. Each packet had a match pasted inside. 'Don't tell anyone where you got them from' was Tegg's familiar warning.

Then something dangerous happened.

Peacock and Bloxham arrived in the ice grey Austin Cambridge. They parked, with two wheels on the pavement, and Sergeant Peacock went into the shop. Timbers could see Bloxham grumbling about being left in the car.

Please, God. Don't let Ned appear yet. Nearly an hour had passed since her phone call to Stuart; she didn't know if the message had reached me. She didn't know if I was caught up with the others and unable to help, unable to get word back to her. But if I turned up now when half of Central's C.I.D. was on the scene, Timbers would spend another night in a police cell.

Bernie Trent emerged, in his braces and slippers, a brandy or something similar in one hand and a cigar in the other. But he wouldn't get in the car. He argued with Peacock on the pavement, both exasperated by the other's stubbornness. Hands jabbed and shook in the air. Hair got ruffled, collars got tugged and stretched.

Henry Bloxham climbed out of the car and left them to it. He'd had his fill. Tomorrow, he would declare that he could work with this D.S. no longer. He wandered up the road, his hands in his pockets, his big policeman's feet clopping on the kerbstones in a lugubrious rhythm. He crossed to Timbers' side of the street and dawdled towards her junction.

Now, Peacock had walked into the middle of the main road. He was arguing loudly that Ned Machray should be brought in for questioning. His name was everywhere they looked in this murder case, he insisted. But Bernie Trent wouldn't concede. The smugglers had slipped through the net that evening but Old Ned Machray was still Bernie's right hand man.

With Peacock drifting towards her, drawing Trent with him, and Bloxham patrolling in her direction, Timbers tried to shrink further into the dark – but she stiffened. Someone had crept behind her. "I'll give you ten bob," he whispered.

It was Berkeley with ale on his breath and his frozen fingertips fidgeting in front of his face. She pushed him away, shaking her head and silently mouthing 'no'.

"Ten bob, Timbers, and I'll put my hand up your skirt while you count to sixty."

"Look –"

"Look, nothin'. If you don't take my ten bob, I'll do it anyway."

"You won't."

"And you won't do anything to stop me, not tonight. Tonight, you'll put up with anything."

"Mr Berkeley, please don't."

"Look, I'm on your side, aren't I? Whispering, aren't I? – So that the coppers can't hear us."

She gazed down at his wrinkled face. Once a tidy old bachelor who looked after himself, Ernest Berkeley had gone for days without shaving and he had blobs of dried egg yolk on his shirt collar. "I'm not what I was," he said, reading her thoughts. "But neither are you. Two old crows spooning in the dark. What d'you say, Timberdick? Are you ready to take my ten bob?"

He chuckled. Sniggered. And Timbers caught a trace of the giggle that she had heard through Smee Ditchen's letterbox.

Berkeley laughed at her. "You're a child. The easiest thing is to fool a child."

"You're Bugger McKinley's ghost!"

"I am. Most nights in the week. It wasn't my idea but I'm mighty good at it, don't you think? Maggie wanted the good people of Goodladies to worry that old Bugger might still be alive."

"Why? I can't understand."

"She didn't want people to think that they were free of him."

"But Maggie never needed Bugger's reputation. She always managed on her own."

"Timberdick, she's a dealer. She'd have made money out of Bugger's ghost, sooner or later. Because, sooner or later, people would have paid to keep the ghost out of their way, or keep the ghost quiet. Or they would have paid up because the ghost told them to."

"Where were you on the night of the murder?"

"Watching," he said. "Waiting for my supper, I was. It was always good of you to leave something hot for me, Timbers. Yes, I was watching." Suddenly, he pressed himself violently against her. He gripped her ear between his mittened fingers, pulling her cheek against his. "He's coming, Timbers. Big Henry Bloxham's coming back. D'you think we should give him a show?"

His hand went up her skirt. Timbers froze as she felt his fingers in their knitting work to explore her. She knew how to keep him out of harm's way but the adventure excited him so much that he began to cackle aloud. She turned him a little, keeping his back to the policeman. She put her head down — and held her breath against the horribleness of it. Neither Timberdick nor Berkeley was five feet tall, but she managed to hide behind him.

"Dear old 'uns," said Bloxham. Then she heard him walking away again. She didn't know how close he had come or for how long he had watched them.

* * *

I was waiting with my bicycle at the far end of the side street. I needed Sergeant Peacock's Austin to be out of the way before I showed myself. The city's police force was eager to arrest Timbers for murder and most of them thought I would lead them to her. Thanks to Piggy Tucker's antics, few people would listen if I took Timbers' side.

Peacock and Bloxham were shouting at each other. I heard the car doors slam and the engine start. Chief Inspector Trent watched the rear lights disappear down the main street, and then he retired to his lodgings.

The figures beneath the broken streetlamp remained. I wheeled the bike slowly along the dimly lit pavement. When I reached them, Timberdick was pulling Berkeley's hair to keep him at bay. Old Berkeley was enjoying it. He giggled stupidly. He said women hated him and he enjoyed it because he hated them too.

I tapped him on the shoulder. "I think you've bought stolen cigarettes from Rennie Tegg, Berkeley. Should we spin your drum?

159

See what you've got under your bed?"

The look on his face said that we would find much more than hookie fags. He backed off.

"Come on," I said to Timbers. "Mr Berkeley wants us to leave."

"Have you got the book?"

I showed her the leather bound portfolio that a shame-faced Stuart had handed to me.

"Let's go," she said.

We dawdled at first, curious if Berkeley would follow us. Timbers looked back and reported, "He's sitting on the pavement. He's got things out of his pockets and counting them." But she wasn't interested. She said lightly, "It's a pity you've got a fat stomach."

"Why's that?"

"You could give me a ride on your crossbar."

When we emerged on the pavement of Railway Terrace, Timbers was sitting on the handlebars, facing the front and holding on with both hands. She screamed like an excited child as I bounced and buffeted her over the uneven slabs. She jumped off and ran alongside. But I couldn't pedal slowly without wobbling, so I dismounted and we walked together. We laughed and joked. We hadn't been so friendly since my return to the city.

When we wheeled the bicycle across the deserted Goodladies Junction, she said, "I think it was Ruby Redinutt."

"She murdered your bloke?"

"No, you plod. It's easy to work out who did that. No, Ruby was the brain behind the cigarette jobs."

"Nonsense," I snorted.

She took hold of the bike as we entered the Nore Road. She pedalled ahead, then pedalled back and circled around me as I followed her lead. "I told her where the cigs were coming ashore. She should have arrested the gang. Instead, the job was cancelled. And why do you think she was hanging around the stew-house on the night of the murder?"

"She wanted to make friends with you," I said, turning my head to keep track of her.

"No. She was waiting for me to leave the house. Then she was going to follow me to the beach. She wanted to know who was

160

intercepting the drop."

"Grief, Timbers. You can't prove that."

"Not a bit of it. And do I care about stolen fags? God, Ned, I'm not a copper's nark."

I saw that we were approaching the junction with Beach Road. "Where are you taking me, Timbers?"

"Three clues," she said as she dismounted. We trod across the road together. "The book, the walking stick and this." She produced the Yale key from her hip pocket. "Oh, come on, Ned. You didn't think that I handed over the real key to Mr Trent, did you?"

"So, you didn't find the key to the Curiosity Shop on the body?"

"Of course not." She waved her secret key in the air. "This is the mystery one." She looked sideways at me as she added, "You knew that all along. Don't pretend."

"The book, the stick and the key," I reminded her.

"They all lead to the house with the white front door. If the girl on the walking stick handle and the girl in the book and the girl in here …"

"You're guessing."

"… If they're the same girl."

"You're guessing."

"Only for a second or two. But I don't see what other guess there could be. Ring the door bell twice, Ned."

"No," I objected. "Not until you've explained what we are doing."

"Really, Ned. You're a dumb plod when it comes to sorting out the facts. Do you really expect the murderer to turn up at the police station and ask to be locked up? The walking stick was missing from the scene and the murderer was the most likely thief. But why would the murderer take the dead man's walking stick? To sell it?" She shook her head. "Hardly worth the risk. Surely, because the stick can link her to the killing. The girl on the handle. Stuart tipped me off, first, but I didn't see that it was so important until I realised that Gordon Freya could have drawn the same girl in his book. Two people are dead — and they both had images of the girl's bottom. The stranger on his walking stick. Gordon Freya in his mucky book. Now, if the key unlocks this front door, we have our murderer."

"But you know who lives here," I said.

"Knock twice, Ned. And if she doesn't answer, I'll let us in."

On the first floor, we walked into a long room that ran from the front of the house to the back. Aunt Em sat on a cane rocking chair looking at the city rooftops through a picture window, without drapes. Her hair was still in the grey and silver turban beneath the glittered plastic hair band. Everything about her was the same. Her pink paisley dress with the plastic belt, the sandals that were too big, even the make up that had been applied when her face was too close to the mirror — she was just as she had looked in the Hoboken Arms. She still looked like a woman who ought to be drunk.

She was aware of us, but didn't acknowledge our intrusion. She went on, gently rocking, vacantly staring, and humming to herself. She spoke only when Timbers was close enough to touch her.

"Ah, the key." Even the resignation in her voice was cold. "I knew that it would be important. And the more I couldn't find it, the more important it became. At first, I thought, 'So what?' So, they will learn that the Walking Stick Man stayed here on the night he died, but that doesn't mean I killed him."

"Until you killed Gordon Freya," prompted Timbers.

"He came to me. I was in the church that night and he came and asked if I knew where the book was hidden. I didn't. Only you and Stuart knew that. And maybe Shannelle. No, it was as if Gordon Freya had been sent to me for a reckoning. I believe that God delivered him to me. I had to kill Gordon more than Mr Walking Stick? You know that, don't you?"

Timbers knelt beside her. "Because he let you down. He broke his promise to keep his drawings secret. He handed them over so that they could be bound into a book."

"A portfolio, my dear. Artists don't do 'books'."

"And before our Mr Walking Stick returned the book, he had copied one of the drawings for himself and had a silver handle made of it. For his walking stick."

The woman said venomously. "He walked in here, waving it around and – and rubbed his thumb over my Lady Jane."

"He didn't know it was you," Timbers explained quietly.

"But other people would. When he walked up and down the town

162

–" She tried to click her fingers but couldn't. "– Doing it!"

I withdrew to the sideboard and, without invitation, prepared a long Gimlet from the array of drinks.

"You followed him."

"No, oh no. I knew where he was going. Darling, he'd already boasted to me. And he was such a fancy do-dah of a man that I got there before him. That evening, I was in the Curiosity Shop before you. I had tea with Maggie McKinley and promised to let myself out afterwards. Instead, I hid in the box room and waited. I heard it all. I heard lovely Layna bind my foolish son to the rafters. I heard poor Shannelle, wanting to go home. I heard the Walking Stick Man arrive – 'What crinkum-crankum goes on here!' he shouted. And I heard the girls asking for the knife."

I asked what Gordon Freya had been doing at the stew-house that night.

"Spying on Shannelle," said Timbers.

"Oh no, my dear. He had lost interest in poor Shannie, so long ago. He trifled. He always did. He trifled with me, and the ladies on street corners, and poor Yvonne – do you remember her? – and he trifled with Shannelle. Half a year, and he was bored with her."

"I don't think that's fair," I said. "When we spoke in the Hoboken, he was still concerned about her."

"Pride," Em said, loud and clear. "He didn't want her, but he didn't want people to think that she was available for others."

I tried to puzzle it out. "So, Gordon was at the stew-house because he was Bugger McKinley's ghost."

Emily smiled. "My dear, can't you get anything right. Gordon would want others to dress up and prance about. You know that, don't you Timbers? But he'd never do fancy dress himself."

"Berkeley's the ghost," Timbers explained quietly. "He was telling me that on the pavement."

"So if Gordon wasn't spying on Shannelle and he wasn't the ghost, why was he there?"

"Because his latest fancy had asked to meet him there," Timbers said. "Dumpy Piggy Tucker. Your very own 'Dumpy', P.C. Machray."

Dumpy wasn't mine, I insisted.

"It was the easiest thing to do," Aunt Em continued. "Killing Mr Walking Stick." She could have been talking about buying bacon. "I waited until he walked into the bedroom and I stabbed him. I remember his eyes – he didn't understand why I'd done it. Even when I shook his walking stick at him, he couldn't see the truth. I was younger, you see, when Gordon had drawn me. Long flowing hair and my bottom didn't look old. Mr Walking Stick never recognised me, you see. I thought that served him right. Dying and not knowing why."

She told me to pour more drinks for Timbers and myself, and we sat on the carpet in front of her, no longer a circle of strangers. Murder does that to people. It gives them a knowledge and an understanding to share. "You've not opened the book," Em said.

I had given so much attention to Gordon's drawings of the girls I knew, that I had passed the others by. Certainly, I would never have identified the pages of Aunt Em. But she was there – across a double fold, posing just like the figure that became the dead man's handle.

Timbers turned the book to the last page and pointed to the signature of the bookbinder. "There, that's his name," she said.

But Aunt Em went back to her picture. Tonight, she was looking at it for the first time in years. She put her wine glass to her lips and let her eyes sparkle over the top. "I was quite a naughty girl," she said.

FOURTEEN

The Poison

My night duty finished at six but I stayed on to cook breakfast for the lads. Twenty- two sausages in two great pans with the lard so hot that it turned the skins black. That's how the men liked it. Faron, the doghandler, used to collect the burnt ends from other plates and make a hash to share with his dog.

Mrs Fitton, the cook, cleaned the lifts on Sunday mornings. They always need swabbing out after a Saturday night, she said. But she was back in the kitchen to do the eggs. Your Ned Machray not being able to get them right. "They've got a woman in the cells again," she reported. "Our Ruby's looking after her but the Superintendent has said that she must be supervised, so they've brought Sergeant Mary from the Esplanade. Proper chocker, she is."

When I said that the prisoner was being questioned about two murders, Dolly Fitton went, "Ooh Mr Ned. I didn't know she was one of yours."

Henry Bloxham was in for breakfast. He was back in uniform but the Sergeant didn't have a job for him. I convinced him to borrow the station van so that we could move my furniture into Shooter's Grove. The Sergeant and Henry were happy with that.

Three other people moved home on that Sunday morning. David Barton went back to his childhood home in Beach Road. He had wanted to delay for two or three days but Harry, the butcher, wouldn't promise him time off during the week. Shannelle's neighbours were just as unforgiving. "Where are you going to live now that Gordon's dead? You were no more than his fancy woman." Shannelle wasted no time; she settled Timbers' argument with the landlady, and told her old friend that they had to live together again.

They gathered Timbers' things in a cardboard box and left the vestry as the congregation was arriving for the morning service. When Timbers stopped for breath at the kissing gate, she saw young Stuart Morrison walk into church with his first girlfriend. She was thirteen. Her father was in tractors and her mother fussed over Stuart with a diligence that Timberdick could never have managed. She heard the mother say that they weren't to hold hands during prayers.

* * *

The first meeting of the Police Dance Orchestra wasn't a rehearsal but a tea party in the garden at Shooter's Grove. Piggy Tucker and I had spent the morning on our knees, cutting the rough grass with shears and sanding rust from an iron table that had been stolen from a beach cafeteria and left to decay. Two Sergeants, a dog handler, a woman from Records, and a volunteer from the Chaplain's list turned up. Four Constables had promised to come but they had been held on shift. I learned from the start that police work was always going to interrupt orchestra business.

This was my first day as Inspector Machray. The orchestra called me 'Sir' and 'Governor' and I was rather pleased with that. My authority –however unlikely it had been earned – meant that I would decide the musical direction of the band. I wasn't going to give that up.

We had our first rehearsal on Wednesday night. Piggy wanted to sit and watch; I said no. She'd make the sandwiches, she said. I said no.

"Well, can I soak in the bath then?"

"Not until they've gone." It was the inaugural session and I didn't want any noises, off set, to distract them. And I didn't want her wandering around half dressed either. "But if I don't hear a squeak from you until ten o'clock, you can have all tonight's hot water."

When the ensemble had mustered in the large classroom, I declared, "We'll need to play a lot of Glenn Miller." Half were happy and half were not, just as I had expected. "It's what the audiences will expect from a Police Dance Orchestra."

A young Constable piped up, "Can we do the Ted Heath version

166

of Route 66? The Rolling Stones have put it on their l.p., so it will be topical."

"Yes. And it'll show people what we are about," another Constable chipped in.

"I could transcribe the arrangement from my Ted Heath 78," said the woman from Records, full of enthusiasm.

"Are you good at that?" I asked, realising what a useful talent she might have.

"Oh, it's so relaxing. Copying out arrangements by ear. It's like doing needlepoint. It's all a matter of regular breathing, you know."

When the young Constable came back with, 'We could give Like A Rolling Stone the Ted Heath treatment. It's a Bob Dylan song,' I knew that I had problems.

We got down to work. 'Drums' and 'Piano' hadn't turned up that evening so 'Clarinet' (from Records) offered to sit at the piano and the guitarist hummed and doo-doo'd the clarinet part as he strummed. It was a roughish start.

Because it was our first time together, the boys and the lady from Records stayed longer than expected, so Piggy was in a sulk before Shooter's Grove had quietened down.

She didn't talk to me for a long time. She filled the bath with hot water and left the door open so that the steam spilled onto the landing and I could hear her sloshing around while I sat in my office.

"What are you doing?" she called.

"Signing off the crew's expenses."

But it wasn't an expense form. It was a letter from Ruthie. She was settling well in the new home and 'Dickie' enjoyed his new station. 'It is very small and very slow. He has decided to think that the baby is his, although how he believes that he put it inside me, God alone knows. Hey-ho. A perfect solution for everyone. Miss you. Ruthie.'

A perfect solution? I folded the letter and tucked it beneath some papers in the desk drawer.

"You and me, Ned," shouted the woman in the bath. "We're on our own now, aren't we?"

I didn't answer. You and me? Those were the words that Gordon Freya had used. They still bothered me. 'You and me, Ned. We were the only ones left for him to talk to. I didn't send him to the Old

167

Curiosity Shop[5], so it must have been you. As good as killed him, you did.'

The notion was preposterous and I had tried to come up with other ways that would have taken him to Widow McKinley's door on that night. He knew that he would find Shannelle inside. He knew that she and Freya had lived together, although she was only a schoolgirl when the dead man had been in the city. He wouldn't have asked questions about Shannelle. Someone must have told him. And if he hadn't contacted Gordon, he must have contacted me.

I laid my fountain pen on the blotter and listened to the sloshing at the other end of the landing. I got to my feet and I walked like a heavy-footed Police Inspector to the bathroom.

She was there, red like a lobster with bits of her floating on the surface. She smiled and giggled like an idiot when I looked at her. She rolled over, tossing water in every direction, and tried to tease me by lifting her hips into the air. When I didn't respond, she turned back again and nibbled the nail of her little finger. She looked discoloured and out of shape and her hair hung down in rat-tails.

I said, "He contacted you while I was away. You were looking after the flat, and you took his phone call. Or perhaps he called on me and you let him in. Offered him tea and cakes and told him everything he wanted to know."

I knew that I was right. She didn't say anything. She just lay there and wanted me to drool.

"But, you are Piggy Tucker. And, being Piggy Tucker, you had to tell him more than he asked for. You told him how difficult things were between Gordon Freya and Shannelle and how he could meet her at the Curiosity Shop."

"He asked about Em, that's all. He wanted to know where Em lived." She pulled herself to her feet. The stale bathwater dripped and trickled off her. "And why shouldn't I tell him?"

---

[5]In '82, my daughter and I researched the shop's history as part of a Sixth Form project. A bill of sale detailed the oak beams that supported McKinley's roof as 'salvage from the famous shop that once stood where Irving Street ends now'. It seems that the sad little shop on the Nore Road may have been right to claim a Dickensian connection.

"And the rest of it?"

"He mentioned Gordon Freya's drawings and I was friendly with Gordon, wasn't I? Just friends, Ned."

I didn't understand.

"Oh, God!" she said, building the drama. "Was I just supposed to take it? Gordon was telling me that it was only Shannelle that stopped him from wanting me. And all the time, he'd got hundreds and hundreds of other drawings of women. And Shannelle? What was so good about her?"

"And Timberdick," I prompted.

"Yes. And Timberdick. Didn't the Walking Stick Man deserve to know about them all?"

I waited for her to complete the story. She stepped out of the bath, draped a towel over the edge, and then sat on it. Her thighs and belly were pushed out of shape by her own weight.

"He said, thank you. He said he wouldn't be back in the city for several weeks and I said, 'Well, go to the Curiosity Shop when you do.' So that he could see what they were all like. All these people who call me Toilet Brush, and ignore me, Ned. Ignore me, Ned, like you do."

"So, why did you meet Gordon in the alley outside? To make sure that he was there, close to the action?"

"No," she said stubbornly. "I went to watch. I didn't know what was going to happen, did I?"

* * *

On a Monday morning, Timbers left her bed while Shannelle slept on. She dressed in last night's clothes and, promising to wash when she got back indoors, she made her way down to the Goodladies Junction.

It was six o'clock and cold. She was broke and hoped that she might catch one of the dockyard workers on his way home from a nightshift. The rain started and she had to shelter against the brick wall of the terraced house.

She hated doing this. Few of the men looked at her as they passed by. Some were embarrassed. Many more thought what she was doing

169

was dirty. Sometimes she wanted to shout at them. Of the men who were curious, most did not look at her face but weighed up her breasts and hips. Not because they were ashamed but because these were the bits that were on sale. When their eyes lingered for more than a second or two, Timbers would shift from one leg to the other. It was like giving the lead a tug to see if the dog would respond. Usually, they couldn't be arsed.

Things had felt better in the Curiosity Shop, but she was back here now. And pregnant.

Old Berkeley was on his way to collect his newspaper. He had his collar up and kept wiping the rain from his face. He stopped on the other pavement, looked at Timbers and then approached her. "Ten bob for my usual?" he said.

"Bloody cheek," snapped Timberdick. "You've only done it once, so it's not your usual."

"Are you going to let me or not?"

TIMBERDICK'S FIRST CASE

Matador Paperback
ISBN 1-904744-33-8

Timberdick worked the pavements of Goodladies Road where the men had bad ideas and the women should have known better. When the local CID loses interest in the murder of a young prostitute, Timbers takes the case on.

It's 1963 and Timberdick's First Case challenges more than her powers of deduction. "Real people get murdered by their family and friends. We get killed by everyone else," says one of the girls.

> *"Fascinatingly original. Full of interesting characters. An array of odd balls gives it almost a Dickensian feel"*
> (Nottingham Evening Post)

> *"A fantastic novel. It leaves you begging for the next in the series"*
> (Montgomeryshire Advertiser)

LIKING GOOD JAZZ

Matador Paperback
ISBN 1-904744-96-6

The city back streets rock to Bo Diddley and Chuck Berry 45's, but the swinging sixties bring nothing but trouble for the cheapest call girl on Goodladies Road. Searching for an abandoned infant, she hears that the father has been murdered. She soon learns that she can trust no-one, not even those who are close to her. Before it's all over, she's sure of just one thing. No place rocks like the Hoboken Arms on a Tuesday night.

> *"Malcolm Noble is once again showing his talent for digging deep into gritty crime fiction in a truly fascinating way. An original, absorbing and compulsive read for all fans of this genre."*
> *(Telford and Wrekin Advertiser)*

> *"Noble reels off a first rate story. Vastly entertaining"*
> *(Nottingham Evening Post)*

The Timberdick mysteries are available from your local bookshop, Amazon.co.uk or from Troubador Publishing Online at

www.troubador.co.uk

or on 0116 255 9312.

Keep up to date with Timberdick's website at

www.bookcabin.co.uk